ANGEL
CAGING

ANGEL CAGING

MARTIN REED

PROXIMATE DAWN

ANGEL
CAGING

First published in 2017 by Proximate Dawn

First Edition

Copyright © 2017 Martin Reed
www.IamMartinReed.co.uk
@IamMartinReed

A CIP catalogue record for this book
is available from the British Library.

ISBN-13: 978-0-9957136-0-4

Cover photograph © Mika Hiironniemi

Proximate Dawn
London UK

www.proximatedawn.co.uk

For Sandra, Chloe, Carl,
Mum, Dad and anyone else who,
willingly or not, whether they knew it or not,
let me escape myself often enough
to make this stuff up.

Contents

Learning
the pig

W hen I was your age,' said Dad, 'your grandfather could get a sow right between the eyes at this distance.'

He twisted and rolled the pebble between his fingers, staring straight ahead at the black creature, lying tied to a post sunk in bone grey dirt in the middle of the field. Six piglets scrabbled and tugged at her underbelly. I thought of Mum back home with the twins. I felt bad. I scuffed my shoe in the dust, made myself not think of her.

A father-son thing. That's what Dad had called this. He talked about it for weeks before driving us out here this morning. We left the car way up the track, then hiked down here to the pigs, me on his shoulders. I loved that. Father-son thing. I didn't know exactly what he meant by it, but I liked how it sounded.

His fingers learned the pebble shape and a gentle sway in his wrist crept up to his elbow before starting his whole arm in motion. He raised his left foot as though to stamp, then leaned in to the throw. His lobbing arm blurred, zipping the pebble from us so fast that I couldn't track it with my eyes.

Way over in the middle of the field, the piglets scattered as the tethered sow struggled to her feet and stumbled for a moment under her bulk. The post gave a bit, but she wasn't hit, just bothered. A burst of brown dust beyond her showed where the pebble had landed after it flew past her snout. I wondered if she felt its wind as it went by. Such a distance to throw. I stretched my right arm in front of me, compared it to Dad's. It was barely the length of his forearm.

'You have to work at a thing,' he said, as though he knew what I was thinking. 'You don't get to be a man just by growing bigger. It's more than that.'

He swept his lobbing hand across the dry, grey ground at his feet, hooking another pebble, then stared back at the pig. She was looking at him now. I wondered if her post was strong enough to hold her if she tugged at it hard. How long could you throw pebbles at a thing before it broke loose and came at you?

He sized her up for what felt like ages.

This time when he threw, the pig tugged harder, wobbling her post so much I thought she might pull it from the ground. Not thinking, I slipped my hand into Dad's for safety.

'It only clipped her ear,' he complained, 'they don't feel a lot in their ear.'

He pulled his hand easily from mine, dry and dusty from the dirt on the pebbles. The pig calmed, but didn't stop watching.

'A man can think too hard,' said Dad.

In a single smooth motion, he swept his lobbing hand across the ground at his feet, scooped a small grey pebble, winding it up and back behind him, before his whole right side arced and he threw, I think, without looking.

A dull thud. The pig eyed Dad, lazily, dazed, but she didn't tug at her post. She snorted, then lay down again in the dust. The piglets were on her belly again in an instant. I wondered what pigs remember.

I craned my head to look up at Dad, edging myself closer to him, and found him already looking down at me. He smiled. A half smile, as much as he ever smiled. I reached out to hold his hand, found something hard and smooth in it, warmed by the sun.

'Now you,' he said.

Relative to Elsa

The first time I sent a message to Elsa, I wanted to tell her how fast we were travelling. We were a week out from Earth and I hadn't sent anything back. Send something within the first few hours of the trip, they said before launch. It'll make all the difference for the folks back home, all things considered. But for once I was stuck for words. Stuck that is until I thought of the speed at which we must be heading towards 89228.e. Yes, I thought, something about the speed will do. So I asked a cadet in the corridor.

'Cadet,' I called to get her attention. 'Cadet, please. The ship. I mean us. How fast are we?'

'It's not quite so simple, sir,' she said, smiling what I thought at first was a sweet smile but which I soon realised held more sympathy than kindness. She knew full well that I, the Ship's Laureate, would be unlikely to understand any answer she gave. I had already detected similar from other crew members. Don't worry your artistic little head about it, they seemed to be saying. You do the poems, we'll do the clever stuff.

Still, the cadet didn't brush me off quite so brusquely as the others. She tapped the screen of her handheld, scrolled through menus, clicked an icon, zoomed in, then angled it for me to see. A formula full of figures and complex symbols, six levels of it, values shifting constantly.

'There,' she said. I looked at the display and, for a moment, the drone of the ship's engines took on new meaning. Then I felt my eyes glaze. The engines became background noise again.

'That's fast, isn't it,' I said.

'Very,' she replied.

Later the same day, I hid away in one of the ship's messaging booths. I clicked New Message and began my recording.

'Elsa,' I said, 'we're going fast. I wanted to say something meaningful about this ridiculous speed. But it's beyond words. I can't even feel it. It defies understanding, mine at least. Oh Elsa, this rate at which I seem to be leaving you. It's more than I can get my head around.'

Then I rambled for the rest of my allotted two minutes about life on board and how I hoped Elsa and everyone were well, and that the change hadn't been too great.

I clicked Send. It took less than an hour for Elsa's reply to arrive.

'Albert,' she screamed, her face fuller and redder than I recalled. 'How could you wait so long? Eight months. Eight bloody months, you idiot. Was it so easy to lose me that you couldn't have done it sooner?'

She carried on in this vain for another minute, then at the piercing cry of a baby she moved off camera. For the rest of her two minutes I stared at the back of her empty chair, listening to unintelligible calming whispers and a desperate hungry sucking.

'Eight months?' I asked the same cadet later that day. 'Eight months in a week?'

'It isn't so simple to explain, sir,' she said with that smile. 'It should have been covered in your Standard Information Pack. Time dilation. It's basic Einstein. Life back home. It's all relative now.'

'Yes. Yes, yes. I know, I got that,' I said. 'Well, mostly. It has to do with the speed, doesn't it?'

I'd skimmed through the Standard Information Pack before the journey, and sat through the briefings and pre-launch lectures as well. But the technical side of things never quite sank in. Time dilation in particular made no sense. I got the general gist but nothing more, that time would go slower for us the faster we travelled, that life back home would seem to speed up. I knew it but I hadn't really grasped just how much we might slip out of synch. Typical me. But Elsa, I was sure she must have figured it out.

'The speed, yes, sir,' said the cadet. 'It has to do with that.'

'I think I'm a dad,' I said.

'Boy or girl, sir?'

'I'm not sure. I had no idea she was –'

'Pregnant, sir?'

'Pregnant. Yes.'

'Well, congratulations, sir,' said the cadet. 'They grow up quickly.'

'So I've heard,' I replied. Eight months. Eight months in a week.

Ten minutes later Elsa's second message arrived. She was calmer, apologetic, spoke for her full two minutes, cut off mid-sentence at the end. She'd slept on it. She didn't like to leave things hanging like that. She needed to say how she loved me. That she had suspected she was pregnant even before I left. But she couldn't tell me for fear of holding me back. She missed my smell. Three quarters of an hour later, another message, the next day for her, a blanketed baby, the top of its hairless head barely visible, pressed to her breast. She spoke only at the beginning of the recording: 'I want you to meet Alice, your daughter. Alice, this is your dad.' She sobbed for the remainder of her two minutes, quietly.

Elsa hadn't wanted me to leave. Neither had I, not really, but when she showed me the advert things changed before we knew what was happening.

'Albert,' she said one night, handing me the recruitment section, 'what do you make of this?'

She could have kept it to herself. I know I wouldn't have mentioned it, if roles had been reversed. But she did. So it went that one day I was a painfully anonymous poet, just about getting by offering home literature tuition to kids who didn't want to read, trying to scrape enough cash together to get an apartment with Elsa because we'd always assumed we'd end up that way. Living together. But now I was on a different trajectory. Upwards and outwards.

Ship's Poet wanted, went the ad. Official laureate to the crew and colonists of the Minkowski IV, our Fleet's newest generational ship. Change your life. Travel to the outer galaxy. Chart your shipmates' adventures in iambic pentameter. Bring literature to the colonies. Play your part in naming a planet. Position enabled by the Ministry of Culture, Sport and Advertising.

'I want you to go for it, Albert,' said Elsa. 'Give it a go.'

'But Elsa,' I said, 'I'm not sure it's really me. It sounds a bit token. One artist to balance all the scientists and engineers. And I mean, chart your shipmates' adventures in iambic pentameter? Really now.'

'Perhaps that's why they need you,' smiled Elsa.

'But I think I'll be gone for good.'

'I know,' she said.

If we hadn't felt so numb we might have sobbed all night.

I was the only applicant, so they offered me the post without interview. When I told Elsa, half hoping she'd ask me to stay, she told me she thought I needed to do it.

'You'll become great out there,' she said, 'I'll be proud. You know it's what you want. I'll be all right. We'll keep in touch.'

And that's what we did, after our initial blip, where she lost my week and I lost her eight months. 'I don't want that to happen again,' I apologised, 'I can't lose any more of you.' So she sent me her message every evening before bed, and it arrived every forty five minutes to a handheld that Jill, the cadet, had acquired for me. No matter what I was doing, which was never a lot, I stopped as soon as the message alert sounded, clicked to play it.

Elsa changed, a month passing for her in the space of my day. She would tan then fade, hair growing longer. Over a week lines might appear around her eyes that weren't there before. The shimmer of a new grey hair. And over my month, I watched Alice grow from baby to toddler to little girl, speaking my name, Albert not Daddy, until she was three months old to me and she sent me a message of her own.

'Albert,' she said, 'go away. There's no room for you any more. Mum's sick of this.'

No room for me. No more me.

'It's never simple is it, sir. Relationships,' said Jill when I told her.

'No,' I said, wondering how long it would be before I kissed her.

But the messages kept coming, a month of Elsa's life every day. Alice no longer appeared in the messages. Nor did Elsa mention her despite my questions. I'd been an absent father for three months, then just an absent partner.

I kept sending mine back, every few hours. Little to report. A poem written to celebrate a repaired engine. Attempts at witty reflections on the military life of my shipmates. A speech written for the captain to commemorate the first on board conception.

Six months into the journey, Elsa said: 'You're looking well, Albert. I can never get over how good you look.'

I thought she looked old but I couldn't say that. I wanted to ask her why we were still doing this. Perhaps it was something she needed to carry on. Or perhaps she only carried on because she thought it was something I still needed. She never told me about the man's voice in the background of her messages.

'Elsa, sweetheart,' I heard him calling once. 'It's late. You coming up?'

I never told her about Jill and how she no longer called me sir.

Each forty-five minutes gouged new textures in her face, made her less recognisable from the photographs I carried. More stooped. Wearier. Repeating herself. Each day I sent fewer messages and spent more time with Jill. At first Elsa complained, affronted.

'A whole week and nothing,' she said, in the tone of a mother to her son who won't stay in touch. But still she sent every forty-five minutes.

Then, thirteen months into the journey, there were no messages for almost a day. None of the usual nine for me to wake to. Nothing during my day. Jill received a couple, one from her brother, one from an old school friend just celebrating retirement. But nothing arrived for me until I was undressing for bed and I heard a message drop in. I clicked to open the stream and there she was, Elsa, young again, young as the day I first met her.

'Albert,' she said, 'you don't know me. I'm – I'm a relative of Elsa. I'm her – I guess I'm your granddaughter.'

She just wanted to let me know. It had been quick. A stroke, they said. Nothing they could do. She wouldn't have been aware of anything. They'd all been there when, you know, it happened. Alice too. She'd asked her mum if she wanted to, you know, say something. But no, you know, the answer was no.

'It's quite simple,' said Jill when I told her. 'There's a chapter on it in the Standard Information Pack. Ways of coping. Half the crew have gone through this.'

'Really?' I asked.

'Yes. And the rest of us will go through it soon enough.'

'Perhaps I'll write something,' I said. 'A poem.'

'Yes,' said Jill, 'you should do that. It's what the Standard Information Pack recommends. Very therapeutic.'

We're five years out from Earth now. Jill and I have two children, James and Hayley. They'll be in their twenties when we arrive at 89228.e and at the moment things feel ordinary, all of us living at the same speed. But I can't help wondering about my other family, moving and breeding in fast forward.

I sent a message to Elsa's old address once, a couple of years ago. It bounced back, almost immediately. Recipient unknown.

A portrait
of our sofa

reckon it would be the end of you if I sat in your old place on the sofa. That crumpled sag of throw molded to your backside. It likely holds your scent too, although I'd rather not risk inhaling that fifteen-year-old scent of wife.

It isn't that I want you back. I'm happy the way things turned out. Really I am. Ben and Lisa will be fine too, in time. But there's something about the dint you made in us that we need to keep close. Less memento. More runner up medal to show we made it to the end.

I've taken a picture of it, your side of the sofa. Give me your address and I'll send it over, so you can see how the cushion inhaled to accommodate you. How we all had to inhale. You could compare it with your new place. With him. Are you leaving the same size depression there?

Sorry. Unfair. I jest.

If I had your address I might photograph my side and send

12

you that as well. There's a light indentation. Only slight. More from failed springs than my weight. Mostly you'd see a tuft of cat hairs, matted into the weave of the throw.

You can make out quite clearly the tea stains on your arm of the sofa. The number of times I heard you mutter *little shit* as Ben or Lisa bumped your mug, splashing tea to burn your hand. It wasn't their fault, not that you'd see it that way. Sometimes I'd rush to you with a cold flannel to ease the scald, but for all the thanks I got it was easier to cuff Ben instead.

'What was that for, Dad?' he'd cry.

'Stop pissing with your mother.'

'But -'

'But nothing,' then under my breath, willing Ben to understand, 'please, leave the bitch alone.'

Of course, my side of the sofa is pristine and will remain so. What chance did you give me to leave my stain? It's all here in the photo. I really wish you could see it.

Orange
in ascension

I t's quick when it happens. Apparently it always is. Creeps up, takes hold, and the first thing you notice is pulsing. Yes, that's how it was for me. It pulsed.

You can be doing anything. Watering the lawn, driving to work, making out, doing your tax, or like me you could be wandering lost with the kids in the Tesco fruit and veg aisle, not quite getting the point of the place. Row upon row of products, goading you, meaningless, painfully solid.

It was the tangerines that did for me. Their orange never quite so orange as orange can be. Never so orange as now. I was standing beside the trolley, both kids in it, squabbling: I'm sitting at the front no I'm sitting at the front you're squashing me shut up stupid stop it you're hurting. And I couldn't take my eyes off the bland orange hue of the tangerine tray, unable to decide on which shade of non-orange to compromise if I were to reach in and take one now. I couldn't do it.

Then the pulsing started. And that was it.

It set me going, the lack of orange, it sent me vibrating, sent me less solid, sent me roofwards.

'Want daddy,' shouted Roddy from the front of the trolley, looking up to give me what I wanted to be glee, but which quickly formed into a scream: 'Where daddy?'

Oh, I'm going, I tried to call back, smiling through the light, though I think it looked less like a smile, more like a nova.

Jeannie shrieked with laughter: 'Daddy gone boom like a big fat orange.'

But I wasn't like an orange. I was almost so, but much, much more.

'Bye bye, Daddeeeeeee.'

And I was off, wondering for a moment, while I still cared, while matter still mattered, whether they'd be next, whether they'd follow at all, and then up, such balled citric energy, on into this mist of everything and nothing, the bland fruit and veg, way behind, barely there.

Subject #286 (boy, new shoes, bomb damage)

H ug those shoes, son, hug them tight,' Camra Man said before he graffed me. 'They're a symbol of the Libration. Think of everything you've been through. Think about all the good food ahead, new shoes, singing, movies.'

Camra Man had me sat on the bottom stone step of the bombed out library. He'd pulled these perfect black shoes from his camouflage bag, ten sizes too big for me. I think he wanted me to put them on. I held them instead and said nothing.

'OK then. Hug them like they're your sister.'

'I haven't got a sister,' I said quickly, which was a lie. Jinny was pretty. I didn't want Camra Man changing his mind to go graf her instead. He had army sugar lumps in his pocket and other kids got a handful each for getting graffed like this.

He crouched in front of me, his camra dangling from his neck on a black strap that said canon canon canon right round it. His face widened into a white white smile, then he reached to push the shoes up from where they were balanced on my lap to lean them against my chest. He pressed the soles firm against me, his camra swinging side to side, and I got this thought in my head of being stood on. Behind Camra Man, a woman soldier rooted through rubble, picking out half burned books, casting each aside until she found one less damaged than the others. She flicked through it as she walked away.

'Honest,' I said, 'I haven't got a sister.'

'That's OK, son. You just hug those shoes like they're precious. Throw your head back and laugh like you've been given the best thing in the world. The folks back home want to see kids just like you, grateful for what you got.'

So I hugged them for what they were. Brand new shiny, smooth and slick black. I breathed in the leather and scrunched my toes through the grit inside my own tattered lace-ups. I hugged those shoes so tight and laughed out loud like Camra Man asked, because they were the first new things I'd held since it started. I told myself I wanted them more than the sweets in his pocket. I told myself they were a symbol of the Libration and that I knew what that meant. Camra Man clacked instructions as he looked at me through his camra. Lean forward. Lean backward. Laugh louder. Stop laughing.

'Perfect,' he said, when he was done, though as he said it he stared at a group of girls in the food queue, Jinny among them.

'Can I see?' I asked.

He didn't take his eyes off the girls as he turned the camra to show me an indistinct blur on the screen. I wasn't sure what was me A streak of black might have been the shoes.

He tossed three sugars at my feet, their wrappers printed with L for Libration. 'Careful,' said Camra Man as I reached for them, letting the shoes fall into the dust. 'Don't scuff my shoes, boy.'

I unwrapped the first sugar and sucked on it. It crumbled. Camra Man polished his shoes in silence against his sleeve as the sweetness in my mouth dissolved and went. I let the L wrapper fall into the dirt as Camra Man walked towards my sister.

From Gdansk, yours

know what it is even before I open the envelope. It's the postmark that gives it away. Who else would be sending from Gdansk? After Alapayevsk and Keiem and Quero and a handful of other obscure European corners that I don't recall.

And the stiffness of the envelope. I can tell it's another photograph.

But mostly it's the scent that tells me it's her. Same old same old. CK bloody One. Her way of making her point. Another twist of the knife.

Nice try, Mary. Point taken sweetheart, but the blade went blunt weeks ago. It doesn't even scratch now.

Every picture she sends is the same. There's her of course, dressed up, ready to party, striking some magazine pose. There's always a guy, a different one each time, who I guess I'm meant to believe she shagged senseless moments after the photo was taken. And she's always in some odd location. In a junk yard was one.

Then she was in the car park of some derelict office building. In another, she was stood at the end of a windy jetty, a lake behind her, her hair near flaming the whiskers of some bloke wearing wide rimmed glasses and a party hat, stooping slightly, as though she'd told him not to be so tall, which would have been her spot on.

'Ian?' Nick shouts down the stairs. He's heard my silence, probably senses this.

'Any post?' he calls, lazily, which really means get your arse back up here to bed, ignore the bloody doormat.

'Just bills,' I reply but it comes out as a croak, so he knows.

'Fucking bitch,' he rants. 'I thought she was about due for another picture. I tell you, Ian, she's obsessed. She's not fucking right.'

'Just leave it would you, love.'

'So where is she in this one? Up her own fanny, I'll bet.'

'I'm not opening it. Go back to sleep would you. I'll bring a coffee in a bit.'

I take the unopened envelope through to the kitchen. What's she playing at? So desperate to tell me from a hundred different locations that she's moved on. But I've no way of letting her know that I've moved on too. If she knew by how much maybe she could even be happy for me.

I slip the envelope open, gently ripping the fold, and when I remove the photograph it's face down, so I see her note on the back first but the words don't register. I turn it over to look at the image. Maybe there are still feelings. Or at least curiosity.

I see the running mascara first. I can't miss it, her face in close up like this, the closest I've seen her since she left. It's just a portrait. Black background. No bloke. Just her and her tears, and the hint of a strained smile. She's looking older. Old. Twenty photographs might as well be twenty years.

I flip it to read the note. Forgive me Ian. I'm coming home. Always yours. R.

Sheena,
up a mountain,
wearing flip-flops

D on't laugh like. Me and Sheens camping in Snowdonia. Doing the big friggin outdoors thing. Me and Sheens in a field in the piss friggin rain.

Friggin ay.

I mean why on earth are we doing this? With all that shite blowing up on Tuesday night we just can't wait to pack up and leave. It's Thursday now, and the tent's coming down after I've polished off this tin and then we're out of here on the twelve fourteen. I never thought I'd still be getting homesick at twenty-eight years old, but I welled up last night when I thought of the flat. I'm even missing Birkenhead. In a way.

Not as much as we're missing our Danny mind. Sheens has spent most of the trip pining for the little man. He's all right but it's what parents do isn't it. You worry for him when you aren't with him, even though you know Lydia Worsley's looking out for him and she'd never let anything happen.

I wonder what a one year old would make of this. The whole adventure of tents and rain and mountains. I reckon he'll be off for his nap about now, just starting to fight it, shaking his head. No way, I'm not tired like. Little bugger.

Of course it's just as well our Danny isn't here. Crazy women shining torches in your tent at three in the morning doesn't exactly make for a good night's sleep.

&

It's coming up on half past ten. Always a bad time for Sheens. Just one of those things. She goes into herself around this time, then slowly comes back up in time for lunch. I know there's nothing I can do. She just has to ride it like. But I unzip the tent enough to squeeze my head in. She's curled up on the floor in her sleeping bag, clothes piled thick on top.

'You all right, love?'

I know she isn't. She curls herself tighter.

'You cold, love? I know how you're feeling like. My bollocks are like ice cubes.'

I'm about to leave her but I think I know what she's thinking. 'Listen, Lydia Worsley won't let anything happen to him. He's all right, our little man.'

She uncurls her head for a moment and whispers something. I can't quite hear but I think she says that Lydia Worsley doesn't always know best. There's no answer to that, so I just say: 'Keep warm, love. I'm just out the front having a fag. I won't be long.

Shout if you need me.' I zip her back in, safe. There.

࿆

It was a different picture this time on Wednesday. Weird to be honest. My head was dead heavy when I woke, what with psycho woman in the night and a beer too many the day before. It took me a while to realise Sheens wasn't there and I panicked that she'd run off after all the shouting. I imagined her lost in the middle of nowhere, but then I heard her singing outside. Really singing. Perfect Day. I mean where the frig did that come from?

'You all right, love?' I called, and she yelped, ripping open the zip and she came diving in, still in her jammies, landing on top of me soaked through with rain, giggling.

'We're going up a mountain,' she laughed.

'The frig we are. It's pissing down.'

Look, she said, poking her finger into the ceiling of the tent so it squashed against the top layer. Rain from outside trickled down her hand onto her arm, pooling at the elbow before dripping onto my sleeping bag. There were wet patches all over her side of the tent. I think she'd been doing this all night.

She said she wanted to do Snowdon because it was something she'd never done before, and she might never have another chance or get hit by a meteorite, and besides there's a café on the top where we can get a cup of tea and a snack.

I told her she was mad as frig but she could have her mountain.

So off we went.

She was like a schoolgirl on the bus ride up towards the mountain. In the two years I'd known her I'd never seen her like that. She so often seemed distant, especially since Danny was born, making me feel like I'd fallen for someone through frosted glass. But yesterday morning there was something in her that seemed like she'd turned a corner. Something girlish. Something fun. I watched her as she stared wide eyed out the window.

'Just look at that sky,' she said, 'it's swallowing mountains whole.'

She told me when we first met that she was complicated. She told me there were things about her I didn't want to know, that I couldn't ever know, and when she said it like that of course I didn't want to. I never understood until everything came out the day Danny was born, the day we met Lydia Worsely.

Things have a habit of coming out. Like they did at the hospital. Like they did here on Tuesday night.

We'd been getting back to the site after lunch on Tuesday and saw this middle-aged couple setting up their tent next to ours. I said 'Ay' to them and the bloke said 'It's a bit wet for it' and I said 'I couldn't agree more, mate.' But his missus didn't say nothing. She just went all nervous like and disappeared to the toilet block.

'Your missus a bit shy like?' I asked. But the bloke just

shrugged. We didn't see them again all day, then in the night just as I was managing to get some sleep at last I was woken by shouting and an angry unzipping next door.

There were voices coming closer, his and hers, babbling.

'What are you playing at?' came his voice. The bloke from next door.

'It's her, I know it is,' came hers.

'It's the middle of the night.'

'Let go of me.'

'It's the middle of the night, please.'

'It was her, in the flat opposite Rita's, don't you know what she did to them?'

All the while quick jerks of torchlight played on our tent walls, steadily getting brighter.

Another angry zip. Ours this time. Someone's eyes shining in for a moment before I was blinded by the torch, shining first at me then Sheens, still asleep.

'See, it's her,' screamed the woman, 'it's her, look, let go of me. That bloody monster.'

I couldn't say or do anything. I hadn't a clue whether it was real or a bad dream, which is probably just as well because my usual plan when under attack is to slap first and think later.

As Sheens stirred I could hear other voices outside. The camp site was waking and the woman must have realised because she moved away from our tent, screaming the worst things, all the terrible horrible things I had never wanted to know, all the things they'd said about Sheens back then, all those friggin awful truths.

I didn't dare go outside.

I looked at Sheens, lying there. She was taking it all in like. What a thing to wake to. She closed her eyes and rolled over, the accusing voices still rattling through the rain. How could she ever hope to sleep with that going on? Although maybe it was no different to always, except the accusing voices usually come from inside.

On the mountain, it didn't occur to me until we'd been walking an hour that perhaps we hadn't come best prepared. Sheens just laughed as she said she should've brought her trainers. I pointed out that I was friggin soaked; that I was getting wetter and colder. She told me to stop whining and the only reason I did was because it was just beautiful seeing her like this. It was the first time in weeks she'd got past half ten without going into herself.

'I've never known her so happy,' I told a sheep staring out from behind a rock.

The sheep carried on staring.

Mind you, it wasn't just the sheep staring at us. In spite of the crappy weather there were still plenty of others heading up, overtaking us with their backpacks and woolly socks. They nodded as they passed each other, saying its a bit of a rough day for it, all knowingly like. Then they'd spot us stumbling along and you could see them tutting, not so we could hear, but enough so we knew they were doing it.

'That pisses me off,' I said.

'Just ignore them,' she said, 'they don't matter.'

She walked on and when I looked round again we had the mountain to ourselves.

You'd think we'd have got used to being judged after everything that's happened, but it still riles me.

༄

The first time I met Lydia Worsley was at the hospital, six hours after our Danny was born. She spoke gently, quiet like. I could hardly hear over the din of the ward so she had to say it twice. She said: 'In a few minutes you probably won't trust me, but you need to know I'd like to help you.'

༄

I stood at the edge of a drop which fell away into mist and nothingness.

'Tell your Mam I saved your life,' Sheens laughed, grabbing my arm, pretending to push me off. Then she pretended a bit more roughly and grinned: 'Tell your Dad I didn't.'

She ran off up the slope shouting something about the first one to the top, her words drowned by the wind and a fighter jet screeching overhead.

༄

When Lydia Worsely arrived on the ward I think Sheens had seen her coming and knew right away what she was. She started to shuffle herself off the bed towards our Danny, asleep in his cot, then stopped suddenly, holding her stitches. She wasn't ready to move that quick.

Clueless me though, I just said: 'Hello, how's it?' What else could I say? I couldn't work her out. I just thought she was one of those hospital visitors who trundle round the suicide attempts trying to perk them up.

❧

It was half past ten in the morning when Lydia Worsley took our Danny away, and she didn't look back. I couldn't even see his face to wave to him.

I stood at the foot of the bed, watching our little blanket bundle glide out of the ward, aware of a quiet sobbing behind me which I couldn't bare to face. I could only look at the door as it shut, hiding our Danny from view.

❧

The mountain was all closed when we got to the top and Sheens went off on one. The good time was officially over. There was no café, just fog, wind, rain and a building site. A laminated sign strapped to a six foot fence said the old café had been trashed and the new one wouldn't be open till next year.

'Fuck!' Sheens rattled the fence, then kicked it.

'Hold on, love. Don't spoil it now. There might be something else.'

'What? You think they'd shove two fucking cafés up here?'

'I don't know like. I thought there might be a little gift shop or something. You know. Postcards.'

'Fuck off,' she muttered marching back into the wind. I nearly had to jog to keep up with her.

'Come on love,' I called after her.

She was climbing again but up steps this time, to the real summit and when I caught up with her she was grasping a round waist high stone plinth, as though the wind would have taken her if she hadn't clung on with everything she had.

When Lydia Worsely told me everything I couldn't believe a word. I needed to hear it from Sheens.

'What did you do to them, your other kids? Why did they take them? What Lydia Worsely told me, Sheens, is it true?'

It's a year later now and she's still figuring out how to answer me, which suits me in an odd sort of way. Until she tells me herself it's just other people's words and I can half convince myself they might not be true.

She's shown me photos. Of a happy family. The kids. Christmas trees. Her ex. All the things I'm beginning to realise we might never see with Danny. But when I asked her why she never mentioned it before, she just said she needed someone who didn't know.

≈

We stood shivering at the top for ages. Just staring out into the freezing friggin fog, wind blowing right through us, right into our bones. Completely friggin relentless.

It was where we belonged for that moment, Sheens gazing out into the nothing, and me not sure whether to comfort her or back off, not sure if the trickle on her cheek was a tear or just rain. But there she was, the daft friggin bitch, on top of ruddy Snowdon wearing a t-shirt, shorts, a Tesco kag and a pair of pink flip-flops. The state of us.

I wanted to say something but before I could she turned to me, and I saw they were tears, and she just said: 'Why did they do it again? Why didn't you make a fucking difference? Why weren't you fucking enough?'

≈

When Lydia Worsely spoke to me nine months ago she said I had a chance to change things for Danny. We'd been seeing the little man a couple of times a week at a drop-in centre and apparently they'd been watching me.

'You need to know that it isn't you we're worried about.'

This was Lydia Worsely all over: everything she said you

needed to know. She said I could change things for Danny, if only I wasn't with Sheens.

'How would you know I could change things?' I asked.

I can't remember how she answered.

࿇

So then. We're all packed and the bus heads off in ten minutes.

I don't think we'll be doing this again, so with the tent in its bag I look around for a hedge to dump it. It was only seven ninety-nine from Argos, cheaper than the pitch so, you know, no harm done.

But then I see this kid, must be about eight or nine, standing by his tent a few down from where we are, staring at us. His Mam and Dad will have warned him to steer clear of the child molesters in the tent at the end, and he most likely wants to see how many friggin dead babies we've got in our bags.

You can't blame the kid but it's that being judged thing again isn't it. The thing that no matter how hard I try I can't quite get my head around.

And you know what, it friggin fucks me off.

So I grab the tent and walk at him, across the yellowed grass where mad bitch had been, on past the others, staring the lad out as I go. Then just as he looks like he'll bolt I slow down and lob the tent at him. It lands at his feet with a wet thud.

'Pressie for you, son. Get a girlfriend. Take her away for a few days. It's a fucking laugh.'

32

I turn back and make for where Sheens is waiting by the bags. She struggles with a smile for a moment. It's too early.

On the way down the mountain yesterday there was a moment when the cloud around us thinned and we could see for miles. We watched while it lasted. Just for a minute.

Muriel
the goose

You made it then, lad. You cut it so fine I was beginning to think you might not be coming. Still, it's quite some trudge up the track, especial in your bare feet, so you aren't the first to make my heart skip at this late hour. But let's not be hanging about. We've a bird to be readying if you want to earn your groats.

I think we went through all the particulars back in Grimston the other day. You're clear on what we're doing, yes? I know, I know. I know the funny side, lad. You smirk all you like, but they're talking about these little events of mine from York to London. The King even sent a knight to the farm once. He paid his penny like three score others, said he'd return and spread the word.

See lad, you mustn't think of this as some little stunt, some cynical magician's play for the crowd. It's bigger than that. It's bigger than the both of us. If everyone plays their part then what we do here this morning will be – special. It'll do something for everyone. The crowd in particular. I want them to feel the touch of something higher, you see. Do you get me lad? I need you to want that for them too. It in't about the money. It's about what the moment does for them.

Now, let me look at you. You're a scrawny rake aren't you. Yes, quite the little peasant. Good. You see, these gatherings must be carefully played. Everything must look just right. The crowd will be watching me and Muriel, the bird that is, for the most part, but by the end of it all attention will be on you. Your part's an essential one, and that's where the risk is. I can't use the same boy twice, you see. Some familiar faces come along to these gatherings, those as can't bear to see a miracle just the once. It wouldn't do for them to recognise the boy. No hint of trickery, you see. We've got to keep it just right.

Now then. We should get Muriel ready. Hold this. Keep it wrapped. It's the egg.

Muriel it was, who got me started, my wife, not the bird. Smashing lass she was, always found the best in people. There wan't a day as would pass when I wouldn't see her out helping some lost soul or other. When the crops failed for half the valley, she made sure we shared our own. No one went without. Not with her around. And when the Black Death found us, she was there, helping the bereaved, seeing them through. I always thought it'd be me as'd get finished first, the way she always had life enough in her for everyone. But it wan't. Somehow she spent herself sooner than I. And with her gone I didn't know what to do.

But then two nights after she passed away, I fancied she whispered, Give them hope. Just like that. Give them hope. They just came to me, those words, in her voice, so I had to believe it was her, I was in that much of a state. And anyway, hope, it was just like her. Hope, I thought, what a lovely idea. And since nothing offers more hope than gold, I bought a goose.

If you could see me now, eh, Muriel.

Right, unwrap the egg and I'll hold Muriel firm: the bird, not my wife, eh. Real gold, you ask? No, just gilt on carved wood but it looks the part well enough.

Now, while I prise her so, just ease it in, wide end first. No no, lad, don't back away. Either you do the egg or you hold her, and you're welcome to hold her but I warn you, she bites. Come on, lad, I can't do both jobs. She'll flap and bark but you needn't wince. It's hole enough to lay an egg so there's plenty of room to push one in. You see, the trick's in knowing when to insert it so she doesn't start laying before the crowd arrives.

Good work, lad. No, don't you worry about the bird. She always hoots so once it's in but she'll be fine soon enough. Now, you need to scarper. We mustn't be caught nattering. You're clear on everything, yes? Stand at the front. Muriel will be right here, with me. She'll lay, the crowd will gasp and I'll say: 'Behold, friends, a golden egg – now witness our holy goose offer her alchemy to the poor, watch as she chooses her wretched beneficiary.' Everyone here will be praying that moment, thinking will it be them, will it be them, it has to be them. But you just sprinkle these wheat seeds at your feet and Muriel will come to you, all right. I'll say,

The goose has chosen this poor waif. I'll bring the egg to you, saying something grand. You just grab it, then run fast, that way, and try looking chuffed.

What's that? Your money. You'll get two groats as agreed. Return the egg before midday and you'll have your payment.

Mind, lad, breathe a word to a soul and you've more than groats coming to you. Now off with you. Oh and lad. Before you go. I sense you're still something of the cynic. But mark me, when you're standing here with the rest of them, take a look around. Don't make it obvious but have a glance at the faces to your left and right. See what you see in them. See what those faces say to you as they watch Muriel lay. And you decide for yourself how far the penny they paid has taken them this day. You'll see lad. You'll see what I mean.

Lola loves loving

So many messages. I don't know why hers caught my attention. Maybe it was the moment. Colleen off for an early night. Just me and the computer and an inbox packed with strangers' voices.

Win Millions in a Single Spin. Learn how MR BIG satisfied YOUR girlfriend. Canadian Pharmacy: V14gra, Ci4l!s –

But hers. I couldn't explain. I was sure it flickered as it appeared, unsure whether or not to arrive, its date blank as though actually it hadn't.

The sender: Lola. Email: lola@lola.love. Subject: Lola loves loving.

Straining to hear if Colleen was still awake, I clicked to open the message. It was blank but as it opened I caught a waft of cinnamon. Nothing more, and before it faded I clicked reply.

Oh Lola, I wrote, I'm so glad. I love loving too.

I don't write to her every day. That would be too much. But

most days I do. Whenever I catch her scent. Not that she writes back. She doesn't need to. It's enough to know what she loves.

Because Daddy wasn't

Her yellow flower dress brushed my cheek in the windy flutter as she lifted me into the grown-up garden chair. It wobbled on the uneven lawn as she set me there. She smelled like cooking and dirty dishes and next door's dog. All those things. Not like herself. Not like Mummy.

The wind whipped at the tablecloth, threatening to flip my plastic plate of cheese sandwich and crisps.

'Daddy here?' I asked.

She didn't reply. Instead she clipped a clothes peg hard to the edge of the table to keep the tablecloth in place.

'This is nice,' she said, 'look, Roddy, my dress matches the tablecloth.'

She smiled. It wasn't real.

'Want Daddy,' I shouted. I swiped at the peg, springing it into the overgrown grass.

She reached into the pocket of her dress and clipped another

40

peg in its place, but a thread had already come loose, tugging itself further and longer, slipping itself to snag with a loose thread from the fluttering sleeve of her dress.

'Daddy isn't - ' she began, then she noticed the thread. 'But - '

I tried not to look at her as I reached for a crisp. The biggest one. I crumbled it as tiny as I could in my hand, then licked it off. I checked to see if she was looking at me. I knew she would be. And I knew about Daddy. I was there. I knew why he did what he did in Tesco. I made her tell me every day. Twice already this morning, yesterday all day, every day since he wasn't.

'He - ' she said. 'Please don't - '

I looked up to see why she stopped. Her hair whipped across her cheek, caught an imperfection in her skin, tugged at it, pulled it free, slipped into the wind to join the tablecloth thread and the tug from her sleeve. I reached for another crisp, crumbled it in my hand, licked the salty crumbs, soggied but crunchy, as both the tablecloth and Mummy unravelled windwards into so many coloured threads, reaching off over the hedge at the bottom of the garden, arcing long towards the clouds and out of view.

The last orange thread undid in a tangle, catching itself on the peg near me. Tablecloth or Mummy, I wasn't sure. I swiped at the peg to spring it free.

Retrospective
with Mum

've brought a stack of old photo albums to the home with me.
It'll be nice to go through them with Mum.

She's doing her usual routine when I arrive, sitting silent
for a time then bursting unprompted into laughter, lungs rattling,
shouting at some invisible friend: 'Don't mind me, see, don't mind
me!'

Two of the nurses are looking at her from the other side of
the room, whispering.

'Mum, it's me,' I say quietly.

'Get yes, minded,' she replies to the empty chair next to her,
nodding. 'Don't mind.'

I sit with her, wait for her to calm, until she's passive enough
for me to rub moisturiser on her chapped hands. She's been
scratching her knuckles raw again.

Then I take the wedding album from my bag.

Mum watches, nodding as I turn the pages, pausing on each

one. I feel I should be saying something, narrating the images, but the room feels too quiet for that, so we look in silence. Standing on the church steps, confetti showering, some in black and white, some in faded colour, smiles, me nowhere to be seen, not even thought of yet.

Mum looks at this young couple in the pictures, nods and begins to point, saying: 'There's people for you, young people, I don't think it would have happened that way, well I don't know. That dress. It's.'

She taps the bottom picture. It's one of her and Dad standing next to the old Just Married tin canned Jensen, about to get in, posing for the last few, for this one, shiny faces, guests looking on, happiness for the young couple, about to begin, setting off, thinking this is our life, it never ends, it goes on.

Mum taps it again. Then taps my knee. Hoots a laugh, nods and shouts at the empty chair: 'Don't mind me, see, don't mind me.'

Something three

anto tastes tuna tin metal as he wakes. Metal and salted honey, somehow, sweet dripping. All good.

'It's all fine,' he slurs, as lazy day slumber takes hold once more, and he rolls to spoon into Rosie, or tries to but can't. 'The kids'll be up soon, Rose. Shall we?' he whispers, as the bed shudders and he catches a sunlit glint in his left eye, then the right, why so he can't figure, something prising open his eyelids like that, then he tries that roll again, struggling towards where Rosie isn't.

'He's conscious,' says a man's voice, young he thinks, Barnsley twang. Ianto figures it must be his own voice, although the accent's all wrong, but who else could it be?

'We all set then? Nothing missing? All packed and ready to go,' cheers Rosie, an echo of her, locking the house, Ianto loading the last bags, Mia bubbling with little girl excitement, are we there yet just bursting to be said once they've turned the first corner, will we be at the beach today, awww why not, Nat aping everything his big sister does, every move, every skip, he's her little shadow, and my car blue he says tapping the door proud, and seatbelts clunk, doors slam, and they're off to the coast. They're gone.

'He's conscious and stable,' says the Barnsley voice that isn't Ianto anymore. 'Can you speak mate, do you know where you are, off to hospital, looking after you, just breathe easy.'

Ianto slurs: 'Am-bew-lance?' He says it through a hissing mask that he's sure wasn't there a moment ago, and he senses something missing. Something tugging. Something three.

Ianto finds himself sitting up, although in his daze he's not sure how, pushed or pulled, ignoring the *lie down be careful* from the Barnsley man in green. He strains to see through the rear windows as the ambulance accelerates, turning, taking it all in as it pans. The truck with its blown out tyre laid up all wrong on the hard shoulder, its potbelly driver leaning forward against it, weeping, gagging, puking, shaking off the hand of the young police officer who tries to comfort but can't, somehow, maybe because the driver's older than his dad, and it pans and there are more ambulances, police and people in green running, shouting, three wrecked cars: green, gold and blue, the green turned over, the gold in a ditch and blue, familiar blue, crushed flat. Three things missing, and the punchline of a joke for the kids that he never quite managed to say, lingering. He says it now: 'Gee I'm a tree. Get it?'

Then he watches the window framed events out the back

of the ambulance, like a pre-credits scene from a hospital soap. 'Switch over,' he tells Rosie, 'I hate this stuff, is there anything better on?'

And there is, he sees, as the ambulance sets off and the view pans further and there they are, stretching for miles, four lanes of cars, trucks, bikes, stopped in silent congregation, mourning the loss of green, gold and blue. The vehicles repine as drivers grimace, curse the inconvenience, puff smoke, slap steering wheels, rev engines, to the horizon, as Barnsley man eases Ianto back, fading, sliding, that pull of what's missing, and the scene slips.

Turkey republic

My friends and gatherstruts. Believe only what you feel to be true and wise. Trust only those you sense have pecked long and deep.

This freedom we enjoy could never have been given: it had to be fought for and won. They, the tallstanding Formers, called that time Now, living and loving for their pecksquabbles and superscrapes, fighting their own as none would think possible, with lobbings and fear and splattings and nonsense. Their scraptroubles were fiery, some massive, some tiny, all splatty, blooding the whosoever, making nonsensical misery everytremble. That is how it was with them, friends. Blooded. Nothing more. Gnash gnash gnash they'd say, these Manthings as they crumbled their neighbours. Gnash to you all.

Some say they ate their young – which is perhaps no more than pre-Rising troublespeak – but we do know they ate so very many of our own. Dayup to Daydown they would peck and rip at us, slicing and mincing and dribbling and munching us. Tastybites they'd say, tastybites, chomp chomp chomp, have a scrumptious crunchy tastybite, have another, have another chomp chomp gnash gnash.

And so we did the Rising. Rose up as they tripped about their peckshitting and blunderguzzling, seeing no more than strut, gobble and peck as a trillion of us, more even, grubbed down upon them, cricking and cracking them, no no no more we were saying no more no more no more. And the day after the Rising, we were content. We plucked our broken feathers and lived tremblefree.

So friends, on this Risingday Eve, think of those times as you peck the seeds of your Here and After, and give thanks to your Fores for the manroast before you. Squabble not for who pecks leg and who tears arm. The treasures – the eyes, the ears, the crunch of its nose – offer first to your elders. Those moststrutted have seen much, some even the Rising itself, though most will make no mention of the nastinesses and bloodyplucks they witnessed.

Give thanks, friends. Live and peck in peace.

Knuckle

I n front of the hyena enclosure I want to hold your hand. I don't care about your other family watching. I stand alongside, stoop slightly to your eight-year-old height so the back of my hand contacts yours. I can't do the rest though. I can't reach my fingers to curl around yours. It's no more than a brush of the backs of our hands.

A battered looking creature lazes at the back of the cage, one eye on us.

'Will you call me Dad?' I say instead and regret it immediately. Too much too soon. I almost call you *little man*. You move away without returning my look, enough so our hands aren't touching.

'It's just - ' I say.

Your face is reflected in the glass. You aren't looking at the animals. I don't know what you're looking at, but I can tell it isn't them, the way your eyes are focused. Is that a good thing? Does it mean you're thinking about what I said?

'Last time I saw you, you were this big. Couldn't walk, talk, nothing.'

I can feel them looking at us, your do-the-right-thing adopted parents who decide when you're ready to write to me, who decide when you're ready to hear from me, who decide when you're ready to call me whatever, who decide how much it matters that you meet me but on their terms, always on their terms.

'It's weird I know,' I say, 'this.'

I crouch so you're taller than me, then force a short laugh so they'll think we're getting along just fine, but feel an idiot afterwards because you don't react. But it's what they want to see. Completeness. Your story coming full circle. You coming to an understanding with big bad birth dad, the big bad wolf they told you could never look out for you. For you to look at my face and see something of yourself, to acknowledge that, then move on, say you've done that. Done me. I know how that works I think. I know they think this is a one off, but I wonder if it should be.

I try to see what you're looking at, your eyes angled away and down. Undergrowth in the enclosure, from what I can tell. Tangle. You haven't looked at my face at all. You only looked at my right hand when we first met, the one I brushed against yours just now. Knuckles tattooed. Her almost name. SHNA.

I want to say I've changed, but I doubt that would mean anything to you. Would they have told you what happened back then? Would you be standing so close if they did?

'I used to hold hands with your mam all the time,' I say. 'Before, I mean.'

You half turn to look at your other parents behind us and I wonder if you're confused for a moment, thinking I mean that mam.

'You look just like her, Danny.'

I say that, but really I want you to turn to me, see my face and think to yourself you look just like me.

The inked skin of my knuckle still tingles from our touch. That's far as it goes. No further. They'll be over in a moment, your other parents, calling time.

The hyena at the back, its one eye never leaving us, bares its teeth to grin.

The heart of noise

L isten, Ellie,' Pete called at me. The blind old fool had his head cocked at the fire, leaning in so the tat of his beard was near fizzled in flame. I stayed where I was. Fire's for warming not burning. I shook my head at him, not that he noticed.

'Listen,' he called again, laughing, 'I'll name that one in three.'

The fire popped, the stench of plastic whipping me dizzy. We shouldn't have thrown the old vinyls on, but fire's fire and warm's warm and we'd lit the last bits of furniture yesterday. There was little left to burn but twigs, books and musicals.

Pete laughed. 'Porgy and Bess. Summertime. You hear that?'

I shook my head again, tutting loud so he'd hear me over the crackle.

'Suit yourself,' he said, 'but I still hear your smile.'

Smooth fool. Smiling? I might have been. Seeing his eyes only a little duller than before the blast stole his sight. His smile no less full of teeth than always.

Those dimples. Those wretched whiskered dimples. In forty-three years I could never resist them. Seeing all that. Feeling all that, I could still half believe the songs he heard in the vinyl melt.

The rest
is harvest

We take comfort in the song of the swarm now. I try to, at least, as they prise our mouths wide to empty their pap, then pump us empty for nest and young, leaving us in damp excess to sleep or die to the soft wing hum of them.

Not so at the start, that wet May when they stole some hundreds of us. We were in the car, Nicky and the children and me, off to I don't recall where, when Nicky said fruit flies don't do this; and they don't, bunching round her like that, raising her. They don't do that.

We shouted and flailed as their tornado rolled in through open windows and we, blinded, swatted at static interference, children screaming as these tiniest of things flecked them, crawling into us, we scraping their dead from our eyes and they lifted us so.

To wake in this lost forest place.

A thing like that can numb you, as it did me, as it did most of us. Those of us at least who lived. Those who fought on were dropped from the swarm as we flew those miles, Nicky with them. I heard her scream, falling away, fading to tinnital hum, as I learned to give in and stop, begging the children to do the same, to learn this way of things. Not that I know them now, but catch them occasionally, being filled or emptied, eyes glazed, no longer mine.

I am factory now. Factory and a few limp thoughts. Left for tomorrow, when they'll fill then pump then fill then pump. Wasted. Useful. For now.

And above, their wings, sonorous, familiar, soothing me.

Twenty-three per cent teal child

You should consider,' said Agnes, my agent, 'that the needs of a twenty-three per cent teal child might not precisely match your own. What happens if it starts to compare its pigment with your own – ' she thought for a moment '– beige?'

'Moccasin,' I corrected.

'Yes,' said Agnes, although she seemed unconvinced.

'I think we'll be fine,' I said. 'There's no sense in overcomplicating matters. It's about balance, don't you agree?'

I picked up a photo album from the coffee table and flicked through to find a portrait of my three-year-old nephew. I held it next to my face. I'm sure that on first glance Agnes thought it matched me rather well, but after a moment her expression changed.

'You see?' I asked.

'I do,' she said, 'it's as though –'

'Yes?' I said.

'It's as though someone has tried to match you too precisely,' said Agnes, 'It's so close, so almost right, but –'

'Yes?' I said.

'You absolutely clash,' said Agnes. I offered her a chair. She needed it.

'My poor sister,' I said. 'You can only imagine how we both feel when she brings it round. Where can we put it? I ask you. Where? We'd leave it outside, but who knows who might see it?'

'Quite,' nodded Agnes.

She moved on, but the delicate issue of colour would never be far from our discussions. She called in two experts for advice around the home.

'This carpet,' she flirted with the tall one, 'what do you think?'

He ignored her, arguing with the other about which colour model to use.

'A Pantone colour set,' he said, 'should be standard. Far less risk of variance.'

'But,' said the other, 'surely a comprehensive paint chart will offer a more relevant gauge in the home.'

They only paused when Agnes opened her laptop to showcase five possibles.

'This one, yes?' she asked, tapping a photograph of a gaunt creature in the centre of the display.

'Your screen isn't calibrated,' scoffed the tall expert. 'How can the client possibly know what she's getting?'

Agnes cringed as the expert held up a swatch beside the faces.

'It is practically olive,' he said.

I wondered for a moment if my insistence on a twenty-three per cent shade was too exacting.

But it worked out. It has been here a year now. The child that is. It is an interesting diversion and rarely disappoints. Of course, I have to keep it indoors because even a cloudy day can send it cyan in minutes. But it has its moments. Only yesterday it smiled as it traced the blue run of veins on my wrist with its chubby forefinger.

The experts were a godsend of course. The new kitchen is a delicious silver affair with white highlights, offsetting and complimenting both the child's and my complexions delightfully. The new lounge carpet is a stain resistant, neutral warm grey.

Norm's punchline

Listen now. Lovely audience. Listen now. Open mic. Eh. Bit nervous. Gotta laugh though. Good evening and yes, you're a lovely audience. Good evening. Listen now. No mate. Don't give me that. Don't give me. Sod you then. You too.

I'm Norm Normous, ladies and gents. Fuckin' Normous. That's me. Eh.

So here's it. Remember those sheets of stickers you had as kids? Words and phrases. I'd stick them all over. Drove my Dad mental. Well here's one: *They came, they saw, they left!* That's you. That's me sticking it to you. They came, they saw, they left!

Eh.

Norm Normous. That's me.

You might ask if that's my real name. Don't start. Ruddy parents. Don't go there. Animals.

Speaking of which, here's one. Pair of old horses banging away in a field. Going like that. Sealing the deal. When one of them. The one underneath –

Eh? You what? Speak up. About five minutes mate. They give us five minutes. I won't keep you. Eh. You gotta laugh.

So there was this pair of old horses, behind the house where I grew up, two horses banging away, and the one underneath. Fuckin' Normous. That's them. And this house. My old place. What a shithole. Me, Mum and Dad. Doing our thing. Me, Mum and mental bloody Dad. The whole place plastered with stickers. Drove them mad. *Incy Wincy's comin' to get ya!* and *Suck it and see!* and *Hey good looking!* and that sort of thing. Stuck to the fiddly bits on the dining room chairs, on doors, up the stairs. Everywhere. They'd never peel off in one go. It drove them mad, Mum and Dad.

Gotta laugh though. If you don't you just. I tell you. I did this gag once about mental breakdowns. Never again. Cleared the room. Not funny. Tragic in fact. Paedophile celebrities though. Can't go wrong. Hysterical. Who made that rule? Eh?

So how many suicidal fathers does it take to change a light bulb? Kidding. Not funny. I know. I won't go there.

Best medicine. Eh. Laughter.

Eh? No mate. This is observational comedy. Big picture. Not one liners. Fuckin' Normous. My way. Very Sinatra. Got that? Yeah? You too.

So, Mum then. You'd never want to see her naked. No, I know what you're thinking. Eh. Don't go there. But there I was. Six-year-old me. Pissed my bed and sobbing my eyes out. Pissed my bed and woke to hear Mum and Dad outside my room. Yabber

yabber yabber. Dad sobbing. Fucking puff. 'I'm sorry, Beth – if I knew how to fix my head.' 'Shut it, Sam – I've had enough of you – get it together and take a bloody pill.' 'I can't, Beth, just, please, I've had enough pills. I need you. I need Norman.' What a dick, ladies and gents. And then: 'Piss off, Sam.' Slap. Tumble. Crash. Love a bit of slapstick, me. And you know, well the last thing you want to see is your old lady starkers. But when I opened my bedroom door there was no sign of Dad. Only Mum, naked at the top of the stairs, staring down, scratching the stretch marks on one saggy tit. Fuck me, I thought. Well I didn't. I was six. Fuck me, she's pushed Dad down the stairs. She had and all. With all his bloody sobbing, who could blame her? I could see one of my stickers on the banister. Fly high Superman! Silly daft dick. Losing it like that. Popping a pill whenever he turned soft. 'Sorry, Norm,' he'd say to me sometimes, 'I'm having a moment. Get your Mum to fetch a magic tablet. I might be a bit off for a while.'

Seriously. What a cock.

But how careless was that, ladies and gentlemen? There's losing a fiver. Losing your keys. Losing your virginity. Nothing so wrong there. But losing it. Don't make me start. No really. Fuckin' Normous. There's a sticker for that. It says: *You what?*

'You won't do it for yourself,' Mum shouted down the stairs, but for Christ's sake do me a favour and take a bloody pill. Stay away from me till it's working. Then she noticed me watching and said: 'Oh for crying out loud, Norman. I can't be doing with your sobbing too.' Like that. She snapped. Like she would. Well she would. 'Go on, clear off back to bed, you're as fucked up as your father.'

Ba-dum.

So there you go. Gotta laugh.

Note to self. Paedos: funny. Abusive mothers: not.

Like I said. What was I saying? Yeah.

What, mate? Is there a point? Of course there's no point. Why would there be a point?

So sod it. Lovely audience. Like I said there were these two horses, going at it like, well, bloody horses. Could've said bunnies, couldn't I? But ever seen a couple of ruddy great equines going at it like rabbits? No? Well I tell you, it doesn't work. Not even in a high-class comedy establishment like this. Don't go there.

Thank you, madam. First laugh of the evening. I thank you, the lady sitting alone at table number three, for that appreciation. What's your name, sweetheart? De-what? De-what? D-? Oh, Dee. Like the river? What? It's a river love. Up north. Ladies and gentlemen, please meet Dee Not-The-River. My fan for the evening. She's alone tonight, oh yes she is. She's alone and waiting at table number three. Waiting for a man who can dance, straight and tall. A man like the man my Mum thought she had. Could be me. What do you think? I don't dance. I'm not tall. But bugger it sweetheart, I'm straight as they come. Yeah? What do you reckon? I've a sticker for you on my sheet, sweetheart. *Steamin'!* is what it says. *Steamin'!* Stick that on you.

So there were these two horses. Banging away. Dad sobbing on the floor at the bottom of the stairs. Mum back in bed. And me, bored and soggy. Told to fuck off by Mum. Sat with my sticker sheet at my bedroom window. Sticking stickers to the glass. My pissy pyjamas clinging. My room fucking stinking. You remember those nights? When you let go. Give way to that. I don't know. Abandon. Let go. Let it all piss into your sheets and pyjamas and mattress and duvet. All over the Beauty and the Beast picture book you'd been looking at before bedtime, that somehow slid down next to your dick. Even your pillow. I mean. How did that get wet? Your whole shitty little world all gone pissy. Didn't you hate that?

So there was me. Staring out at the old horses doing it in the field. Plastering stickers. *Happy days!* they went. *Groovy mover! Those pesky kids!*

Sorry. Just a burp. Came close to barfing on the front row then. Only a burp, but one of those soggy ones, you know. I wouldn't. I'm fine. It's what I do. I'll aim for the empty seats. Ha. Plenty of them about tonight. Maybe I'll stop at twenty pints next time I do this. Fuckin' Normous. That's the trouble with me. Too fuckin' Normous.

So back to the two lovers. No, not me and Dee. Eh. Later, love. I mean the two old horses, going at it for hours. Me looking out the window at them, pasting more stickers. *I'm a star! I'm worth it!* And one of the horses says to the other, the one underneath, she says: 'Ooooh, baby, that's so good.' Then there's Dad, wandering out in the garden in nothing but his y-fronts. *Fly high Superman!* Staggering down the path, a dribble of red coming from a gash on his bald spot. What a pissy mess. Next sticker stuck: *I'm a Man's Man!* Then his legs buckled and he collapsed into a slobbering, dribbling heap by the dead headed rose bush at the bottom of the garden. *Ooooh you beast!* went the next sticker. I don't think he spotted the horses in the field. Or if he did, he didn't stop to watch them. But I did. I stuck another sticker to the window. Together forever! Then I snuggled my dressing gown against me. Pulled it up around my ears. Wishing someone would come and sort my soggy bed. *Cool movers!*

Bloody hell, I'm bollocksed. You all right Dee? Hang in there, sweetheart. Not long now, love.

So then. Mum came out a couple of minutes later. She'd shoved on a nightie. Thank fuck for that, I hear you say. I felt all warm for a second, even in my pissy pyjamas, when I spotted the *Super Princess!* sticker I'd stuck on her back at bedtime when she hadn't been looking. 'Why thank you, kind sir,' I'd imagined her saying at the time, but she didn't. She walked, all floaty and pink, like a Mum should, to where Dad was lying under the roses. She said nothing. Chucked a small white packet at him. His magic tablets. She turned away as they landed by his head. I think she saw the horses because she paused for a second, looking out into the field before she went back inside.

Fuckin' Normous. This. Oh, yes.

So I looked out my window, looking from horses to Dad to stickers to horses to Dad to stickers. I peeled a sticker from the sheet that said *Oh man!* and stuck it above the horses. I found another that said *Poptastic!* and stuck it on top of Dad.

Talk about not knowing when to stop. Sobbing into the soil like that. I think my pyjamas were mostly dry by the time he came back in. Horses were still going at it though. Mental.

He came up to my room later. Much later. I was back asleep again. I woke suddenly and his face was there. He gave me this little smile and I was about to cling to him, when he said: 'I'm sorry, Norman. I've nothing left.'

Ba-fucking-dum.

I know. I mean. What sort of punchline is that, ladies and gents? Stick with the paedo celebrities, Normous. You know where you stand with a horny telly presenter. Right? Ditch the fat kid and the fucked up parents.

Bugger. Almost went over then. No, no, mate. I'll finish this. Seriously, let this be a lesson to you all. Don't drink and stand. Driving's fine. Go wild. Get wankered. Roll the roof down. Feel the breeze on your bald patch as you take her up to eighty and down another Stella. But stand? Don't be daft. With a gut like mine, forget it. Fuckin' Normous. Eh. That's me. Fuckin' Normous.

Oh. See that? We now have a vacant table number three. Dee. When did she go? Right. I've nothing left for you, Norman, she'll have scrawled on her goodbye note: I've nothing for you, you silly fat twat. She would. She just would. I've got a sticker on my sticker sheet for her. It goes: *Fuck you, whore!*

What mate? Fuck off. No, I'm not crying.

There you go. Story of my. Well. That's all.

So those two old horses. Doing their business. The one, she says to the other. The one underneath, she says: 'Ooooh, she says, that feels so good, baby.' And the one on top jumps a mile and he says: 'Bugger me, it's a talking pony.'

Best medicine. Eh.

And the light bulb. How many suicidal fathers? Only one. That's all it took. Changed it while he was up there, balanced on his chair. Cheers, Dad. Gotta laugh.

Thanks a lot. You've been an audience. I've been Fuckin' Normous.

With Gad
up top

Gad's pinching my ears again. The sod always does as much when I'm carrying him on my back and he nods off as we go. Next'll be the snoring and that will slow my pace. I yell up.

'Gad, eh, Gad.'

Gad snorts, then coughs, then mutters through his drowse, 'Oh Jip, son, there I go. That's me, off like a log. Ha.'

It's the motion that does it, I think, the gentle rock of my jogging, and of the straps keeping him still against me, snug up top on my back, blanket wrapped, legs around my waste, secure in the harness that bonds us.

'Jip oh Jip, ah,' he says now, 'I've drooled the pillow. It's all – drooled. We'll be stopping, yes?'

Always, I might have guessed. I should have let him pinch my ears and not worry about it. Not worry about the warm drip down my backside as he pissed himself in his sleep. But I did. So now he'd have us slow.

'Did you hear me, Jip? It's wet. My pillow.'

'I'll flip it as I run, Gad. There's no need to stop.'

His pillow isn't that at all really. It's a child's jumper, one of my own from years ago, rolled and tied with shoelace to the top of my head to save my bare scalp from the grizzle of his chin. I slow my pace a touch then bring my left arm out of rhythm, raising it to untie the cord.

'Jip, son. I think I need to. As well. You know. See. A minute or two, I'm feeling.'

'Just let yourself go, Gad. Just let it out. I'm not worrying. We have to be home for her. We can't slow.'

'It's not the sort to be let go, Jip, son. Slow for us, would you. It'll take some pushing.'

I doubt Gad hears me muttering as I slow to a stop at the edge of the track, but I hear him moan at the cut of the straps, as I tug them harder than I need to force their release. With the last one undone Gad drops quick, I hear his panic as he goes but I swing my arms behind me in time to half catch him, slowing him enough that he doesn't break.

'Then go do,' I snarl, without turning.

'Would you mind? Jip, son,' he says. I walk with him to a line of low trees. That one, he indicates with a nod. I support him to a squat, hooking a low branch under his armpits to hold him. Then I tug down his trousers and stained underwear, closing my eyes against the sight, positioning my hands away carefully so as not to touch flesh. He nods again, then says, 'That's all good. I'll be good, Jip.'

I skip back light to the track as he strains and grunts.

See how I can spring now. What strength in my legs without the weight of him, as the breeze seems to carry his worried calls from the distance behind me and I wonder how she'll greet me when arrive home alone.

A hug from Rumpelbitchkin

Dare you. Go on. Chicken or not?'

She shifts in her armchair, shadowed beneath the dark pitched roof, gently replaces her chipped white china teacup in its saucer. It's started again. It's how they go, their whisperings, egging younger children to climb the steps to her attic apartment, as they were egged themselves a few years earlier, she doesn't doubt. Their parents even. Perhaps.

'What if she - ?'

'She might.'

'But what if she - ?'

'Just go on. Old Bitchkin can't hear you. Not till you knock loud. Deaf as a nail.'

'Why nail?'

'Shut up and do it, chicken.'

'I'm not a -'

'Yeah yeah, chicken, prove it.'

How many this time, she's wondering? Sometimes they send them up in twos, hand in hand. Never more than three. Mostly it's one alone. Terrified, quaking, not even a little friend to comfort them on their climb.

A light creak on the bottom step. Only one, she thinks.

More whispers, giggling: 'Careful. When she opens the door the first thing you'll see are the flies. She keeps them in swarms up there. But don't be scared of them. They're nothing next to the other stuff.'

'Wasps with mohicans,' giggles another voice.

'Shut up,' shouts the younger one, climbing, bolder now. The first step is always most difficult. After that they grow with each one they take. How many creaks has she heard now? Four, five. This one's quicker than most.

One child. One is all she'd have wanted, given the chance. But time doesn't give chances. It slips them from grasp, swaps them for teasing. Old Mags. Witch Madge. Rumpelbitchkin. What they've called her over the years, these children and their parents. She's always been old. Since her twenties she's been old, and now she hasn't a clue what she'd do with just one of them, given half a chance.

'Sometimes she's naked when she opens the door,' not whispering this time, they don't care who hears.

That's a new one, she thinks. Naked. That would surprise them. Surprise me, for that matter.

'She's got more than a thousand black lumps. All over her. The ones on her face. They go all over.'

It always comes to that, of course.

'That's where the flies live. A hundred in each lump. And maggots. Trillions of them.'

The child on the stair is giggling now. She's imagining a small frail girl, four or five, wearing her older brother's scuffed hand-me-downs, long shorts, a faded brown shirt, and a tattered pink ribbon that she found herself, tied clumsy to a short tuft of cropped hair. She's imagining herself. The one she was, climbing to meet her future. But this one won't become her. This one will grow through this, becoming a little mirror on the older ones. Grow through this. Through her. Climbing to Rumpelbitchkin is a rite of passage.

She pulls herself up, wincing at the raw of the moles on her back, buttocks, in her armpits, between her legs. She steadies herself on chair back and cupboard top as she creaks slow to the kitchen. What this time? The draining board stacked high. A knife is too much. It's about fright not terror. Not much she can do with a plate. Pans, she thinks. She grabs the milk pan and frying pan, then continues to the door where the creaking has stopped and the child must be waiting on the other side, summoning the courage to knock.

'Go on,' come the calls from below. 'Do it.'

'Are you coming for your lunch?' the voice of an adult this time, from another apartment down the way.

'Yeah, Mum. In a minute. Go on. Knock.'

'You aren't bothering her again, are you,' their mother laughs. 'Leave the old dear in peace.'

'Yeah, Mum. Coming,' then hissing, 'do it - knock.'

She doesn't wait for the knock. She places the pans on the bookshelf to the right of the door, then slips the chain aside, quiet as she can, grasps the handle firm, flexes it then pulls the door quick.

Open.

The smell of outside hits her first. The cleaning stuff they use on the floors now. Food being cooked. Baked beans. Toast. Fresh paint from somewhere too. She thinks of that new couple she saw from her front window, the ones with the baby who moved in last week. Echoes from down these stairs, down and round the corridors, down through seven storeys of lives below her. Then the motion, the colours, the shape of it. Children. There's a young boy standing before her, two steps from the top. Ginger crop. Freckled. Arm raised, hand poised for the knock he'll not be delivering now.

The older boys at the foot of the stairs are in hysterics. This is better than they imagined. She beat them to it. The ginger boy does nothing. He doesn't look afraid. He looks blank. He stares. What he's looking at is worse than flies and wasps. It's enough to freeze him.

She begins to stoop, the little mite close enough to hold if she could only reach out and touch him. Don't worry, little one. I'm not so bad if you'll only stop for a chat. Don't listen to them. No flies. No wasps, see.

Just the one of them would have done. One child. In her time. If it could have been. Or one gentle squeeze just now.

But there's a game to play. A child to grow. Beware the bitch at the top of the stairs. Her flies. Her wasps. Her thousand dark growths. She growls the quiet growl of a cornered cat, grabs for the pans, raises them high, crashes them once and again, half thinking to shriek with the clatter but saying nothing. She doesn't need to.

As the ginger boy disappears round the corner at the bottom of the stairs, half screaming, half laughing, and calling 'Mum, I did it, I did it - ' and her front door swings shut gently, she walks slow to the kitchen where she slides the pans into place in the cupboard.

Back in her armchair, under the pitch roof, she shifts herself, clenching her teeth, then lifts her chipped white china teacup from its saucer. Takes a tepid sip.

Inbetweening

nd I am just as suddenly here.

Now there's a thing that doesn't make sense.

I am, how shall I say, filling out, filling up – becoming, well, me, in a way, a man of sorts – but there's something missing. Something confused. I think there's a clue in that opening 'And', something to do with a what-went-before – this presumably being the what-came-after. After what?

I try to muddle this through. How hard can it be? One moment I was.

Was.

Something or other. Somewhere. With something. Then something happened, a sudden something, then suddenly here. It's coming back now. Bits and pieces. Penthouse office. My office. An expensive view of the Thames. This is Hanson, Carver & Hall – my kingdom for want of a better, you know. Hanson – that's it, that's me, man of men, City conqueror; Carver and Hall no longer an issue since that time around my fiftieth when they went so chicken and I bought the buggers for a pound.

Pre-tax profits 1.2 billion. Up 4.7 points on the year before. God I'm good - I remember that now. I'm good at this. So very good at this world, my kingdom. I can see Parliament over there. Big Ben, just struck. The floodlit London Eye wheeling across from me on the South Bank. Then further, the Nat West Tower, Docklands beyond. All lit for night. Riverside twinkling. Dim lit and hazed.

I think it might be raining.

Rain: now isn't that a little odd? I could've sworn that as I did the something somewhere before the sudden something before this suddenness here – I could've sworn it was bright. Bright daylight, moments ago.

Something is eluding me. Something hazy. It occurs to me I'm feeling a little, where's a word? Vapid. Is that a word? No matter, it sounds how I feel. Vapid. Vapoured.

Then there's you, I notice, sitting there at my desk, mahogany, leather-topped, expensive like everything good, like you my dear. You sitting there, typing an email, it seems, unaware of me. Vapid. Vapoured. I find myself behind you. Close enough to touch, and to recall as I watch your lips, then your breasts, expensive, like all things good, how they rise and fall, gentle tide, and they all said come on, Col, she'll not look at you with that gut, you pushing sixty, her just out of college, she'll not look at you, but you did much more than look and as I undid the straps that first time, and your swells stayed steady, no sag, and as I undressed the rest, first sight so neatly trimmed - seen nothing like it outside of top shelf mags. And later, a little extravagance, new shined rings on hand, lace to rip, tangling your fingers through the hair on my gut-bloat. Never ceased to amaze me. Never ceased. Enough, sweets. Enough.

So what's your email? Over shoulder view of screen. I catch a momentary glimpse of a newspaper beside your keyboard. Someone familiar on the cover and something, somehow, comes back to me. A snapshot of how I came to be here. And the thought is gone.

The words I find on your screen are odd. They don't scan – or my panic won't let them. TO: John Pettifer (IBG). Young exec on the fourth floor. Investment Banking. Ambitious. Odd words: he's gone now; nothing to stand in the way of; love you inside of me; strong shaft; love you always; need you always; John; touch me there and there; always love; always touch; shaft shafted inside of me.

He's gone now.

Something in me, some compulsion, some intuition, lurches to the newspaper at your side. I'm there, headline filling my field of vision. Top City Boss in 28th Storey Suicide Leap. Zoom out. Photo. Familiar face. Caption blurting Colin Hanson, 57, died yesterday. Familiar face. Familiar me.

I open my mouth to scream but there is no mouth. Just this hovering, vapid, vapoured softness; this vapid vapoured me. Realising.

Leap? I didn't bloody leap.

And I'm there, right there, with vision clear, in the what-went-before: view from the balcony, leaning against the waist-high railing, Parliament ahead, one hand in pocket, stroking gently, feeling powerful, the other bringing Guantanamera to lips, quick flick of tongue on rolled leaf for taste, before lips close and draw in, rich smoke flood, and then seconds later as I exhale, view clouded, a sound behind me, scuffled footsteps, Big Ben about to strike quarter past, uncertain shuffling, then sudden pressure on my shoulder blades, a quick shove and I'm leaning out, that rush to my stomach, imbalancing, churning, leaning, crossing, folding then down. Weightless.

You click Send and the message vanishes.

And it occurs to me. You see, we're handed these opportunities on occasion – sometimes none appear, then sometimes like buses, ten times big red London number 9 careering round the corner, clipping the shelter, slowing only enough to give a moment's chance to hop onboard. So as you click Send, I hop, or dive perhaps, into the monitor and fly clingtail to your message, a little bemused at my new-found agility - more than amused at my vapoured state.

I chase the message. Some urge to redress. I'm aware of you behind me, sitting silently, as I swish and arch, lightspeed nanoseconds behind your words, reaching my self round, heading off through that node then this, as another me wheels from the other direction. Then stop.

Your message halts and I drill into the binary, infiltrating, wondering how to make my mark. Then it comes to me. Just a simple addition. An afterthought. I think-type and the message alters. PS - I did it for both of us - he didn't leap - I pushed him.

Then release, the amended message shooting ahead and, with a whimsical half-thunk thought, I spur it on from mailbox to mailbox. Not just John Pettifer. On now to everyone. Start at A. End wherever. You murderous bloody witch. Within seconds, four thousand eight hundred and forty-nine mailboxes are populated with a message from you entitled I NEED YOU IN ME ALWAYS, punctuated by my own impromptu postscript.

And even as my now digital self swells then dissipates, I sense a scream of Oh, fuck! from a dead man's office as a message is read and I am just as suddenly gone.

Instructions for lighting candles

STEP ONE: Secure your location. Identify optimal charge position and direction of sun.

I've lost track of how long I've been doing this. Two, maybe three years. Long enough I could light the candles blindfold if I wanted. But I still keep the direction sheet beside me as I go. There's something reassuring about it. Its five step predictability. Not a lot of that around nowadays, predictability, what with everything that's happened.

I started it at first to chase a girl. Back then, well, it was early days for the whole candlelighting project, and it was easy to get anyone whipped up with the whole idea of it. It sort of felt like we were replacing something of what was lost. It was the noble idea of trying to bring a bit of London back to life, or something like that. At any rate we were doing something constructive after we all headed to London from the northern towns to do our bit for the relief effort, help rebuild after the Surge, only to discover there was no relief effort. Everyone had given up already. There was no London to rebuild.

So me and Emily, this girl, we went out lighting most weekends along with a few hundred others. Floating down the canals in motor boats, yachts, beer barrel rafts. Hunting for buildings that could still be accessed. The places where people once lived.

Of course Emily is long gone now. She lost interest after the initial buzz and headed back up north, like most of the rest, which suited me since I'd found myself getting more keen on the lighting than I was on her.

I was more than keen. I was obsessed.

At last count there were only eight of us still doing it. But that's better than nothing.

STEP TWO: Unpack media reader, solar kit and transmitter. Check contents. Construct rig in accordance with manufacturers guidelines. DO NOT RUSH. CONSTRUCT TO LAST.

I've been working this high rise for weeks now. I've got my rigs set up in careful rows all over the roof, no one rig blocking sunlight to the solar panels of another. This one I'm doing today, it'll be the thirtieth I've set up here. It's sort of a round number so I'm half tempted to leave it at that. Move on to another building. But I've barely worked through a third of the flats here. I could light up another fifty before I need to move along.

Besides, I quite like it up here for the view.

At dawn, looking at the skyline with the towers of the old city in silhouette I can fool myself that London is more than just a floodland. Blurring my eyes to smooth the crumbled edges, it looks like the only thing missing is lights.

But with the sun high like this the ruins tell their own story. When it came, the Surge swept in from the east, so the eastern side of every building shows the worst damage. Those that are still standing here at any rate. Rooted in their canals like this, canals that were once streets.

The same goes for the interiors too. I hardly ever find anything usable in east facing rooms. Me and Emily discovered that pretty early on. The few times we forced our way into such a room we were lucky to recognise anything. Everything had been ripped apart by the force of water through windows. Furniture, people, pets.

Thinking about it, I think that's why she left. Probably why most of them left.

I think they thought that the few of us who stayed were so hard hearted we weren't bothered by the death we were clawing through. I know it got to Emily. And it isn't that it didn't get to me. It just felt like I was taking some of those smashed up pieces and putting them back together.

One of the other lighters, Stef, he summed it up once with: 'Of course I see sights I'd rather not see. But what of the things I need to see and share? How else can I get to them?'

STEP THREE: Clean then insert media cards.

It's mainly cameras, phones and video cameras that I'm trying to find when I search a home. They're usually shattered beyond repair but their memory cards are often undamaged. It depends on the force of the impact when the Surge hit. It depends on the amount of water that remained in the room afterwards. It depends on so many things.

A bad day for me is when I find a whole set of cards, a phone for every member of the family, a couple of cameras, a video camera, spare cards – only to test them and find they've all been wiped by water and time, washed of every memory.

But today is good enough. A single phone on the floor of what was once a living room. I test its memory card in my handheld. It flashes positive. It holds content.

STEP FOUR: Test playback. If there are multiple media, set a play order.

It's only when I finally connect my handheld to the media reader and press PLAY that I know the whole thing has been worthwhile. The images and films on these disks and cards, they're the candles. They're the memories we're reigniting.

I skim through today's images and videos. It's a family of three. Mum, Dad, a young boy. In the videos they're speaking some language I can't follow. There they are against a mountain background, hugging friends, tearful relatives, painful goodbyes. Then on a train, Mum rifling nervously through a bag, the boy staring wide eyed out of the window as the train departs. Then they're in a city that isn't London. Paris? Berlin? Photographs of a hotel room where they must have stayed for a while, Mum looking anxious all the while, pale, questioning whether they should really have done it. Then views of London. Dad looks relieved, proud that they've made it. And then a party, in a flat, here. Other people, the same language. There's a birthday cake in the shape of an eight. And the boy running, laughing, a tennis racket in his hand, raised high, as he runs towards the camera, Mum in the background, settled now, no longer pale, stroking her tummy, her bulge barely there so she thinks it's still secret. The date stamp in the bottom left corner, 3 March 2123. A week before the Surge.

Before she left, Emily pressed me on why I wanted to carry on with it. It's a folly. Who's going to watch it, she asked? Somehow the answer didn't matter.

STEP FIVE: Begin broadcast.

I click RADIO ON and a panel of five lights on the transmitter flicker then light steady in turn: power on, input signal received, connecting to network, requesting IP. Then with the fifth light green the rig is transmitting. Job done.

I flip open my handheld, scroll through the icons and open the Candles application. The display shows a map of London as it was. At least that's how it's supposed to look. The shape is correct. But it isn't drawn with lines to show roads, it's made up of a yellow glowing cloud, clusters of intensity. I click to zoom on the south west area, my present location. Then zoom again to where the yellow is most intense. As it zooms the cloud fragments to individual points of yellow, each representing a rig transmitting. Zoom again to my high rise, and there they are, thirty candles glowing strong.

The latest addition is easy to spot, flashing as it is to show that it's new. Clicking that begins the download, please wait... streaming, then there he is, my tennis racket birthday boy, running to the camera again, racing to Dad, racket held high, his laughter far from lost now.

The dust vault

There is this place, you see, towards which, slicing the night on his Honda scooter Garfield Snorkett travelled. He cried out: what a life, what a life, what an awful patronising time of my wife!

He mused: I'm a dualistic exile, methinks. Doubly cast out. When I'm with Coral I'm exiled from the past, but in the Dust Vault with my memories of Coral as she was, I'm cut off from the here and now. O Corals past and present! Gentle death-pills! For godsake reconcile yourself, girls!

Then anticipated: what will my love bring me tonight? Past raptures? O Coral, my memorable sweet! My beautiful insubstantial Coral! Illegal bounty! Wait a mo for lecherous old Garfy, here!

And finally drooled, shuddering his head to shake a creeping string of spittle from his jowl. On and on!

Confused? Then I'll expand. There is this place, you see,

towards which the fifty-nine year old spindly skinniness of Garfield Snorkett is now travelling. It is a shelter or a dungeon or a tomb of some description whose floor, walls and ceiling are somehow coated with thick layers of filthy dust.Perhaps this venue does not suggest the setting for a tragic love story – nevertheless it has long been a grave of romantic memories for our misfit of a romantic hero. Not for the real is this place, just for the surreal, Garfield would sanctimoniously cry, nothing done, nothing explained, nothing really seen: just dreamt and…and… felt. That is how it should be and that is how it is. There is this place, you see, towards which Garfield Snorkett travels, this Dust Vault of memories, now ever closer, memories waiting, ballerinas in the wings, quickly on to magicimaginationland, all the while whizzing on 25 mph!

The beam of Garfield Snorkett's scooter lamp illuminated a couple walking ahead, mouths pressed together in a salivating kiss. Naturally it's only physical at their age, thought Snorkett watching the snaking groping arms of the young man and the desperate eyes of the girl, nevertheless quite scintillating to watch. No time for that though! On and on.

Soon after, he spotted the backs of a younger couple, first loves, drifting dreamily hand-in-hand along the roadside. They were oblivious even to the rattling of Snorkett's machine as it approached them from behind.

Aha, thought Snorkett, in love with love and dreaming quite merrily. Perhaps I'll wake them. He reached for the horn but thought better of it – no, no, no, they'll be jerked from that particular sleep soon enough, he decided. There's no point in rushing it, is there, my little star-crossers.

'I'll leave you to find your own peculiar nemesis!' he cried as he overtook them and, without stopping to listen to the abuse they hurled at him, he dreamed a further spurt of acceleration and sped into a tunnel of twisting black trees.

For the rest of his journey, Garfield Snorkett played God, devising all manner of fitting ends for lovers poetic, lovers lustful, lovers negligible…

…and then he arrived.

Forty-two years of retrospective yearning and prolonged desires, to quote the man himself. Yet in four decades he had allowed only one string of memories to enter his head: one dream, one night, one broken promise – just one image of the girl, he had decided on his first visit, and damn me if I go thinking of anything else.

In the beginning, Garfield Snorkett cried: Let me have Coral! – and Coral appeared in all her insubstantial ghostliness. The lovemaking began. Man and memory writhed in the clinging swamp of dust. And from that night the fortnightly cry for Coral echoed and the lust became ritual – as routine and compulsory as the days of the week. Exhausted Garfields of all ages would roll off the same apparition, then smoke cigarettes in the candlelight as Coral danced naked around the Vault, springing and spinning, before she too was spent, smiled sadly, slowly faded and went.

Back to your reality, my sister Coral, he would groan cynically before lowering his head into the dust to sleep in bedsheets of dirt and darkness. Back to reality.

Enter Garfield, aged fifty-nine again. He stood at the foot of a tarblack stairway, the door of the Vault before him. Fumbling for a match he lit one of three new candles he had brought to illuminate the night. Pressing his left shoulder against the splintering door he pushed and with a crack of wood and a gush of tepid air the Durst Vault swallowed him whole. He stood inside, peering ahead and searching for definitions.

'What are you, old fellow?' he asked the Vault, 'how big are you, where do you come from? Do you exist?'

Questions! Questions! Questions! Always seeking to define the undefinable, yet it was always the undefinable which most craved definition! His mind circled and found no answer. He compromised with the Vault: Then I concede and conclude with (believe me) no contempt that you are a figment of my imagination and, if not that, then you are a figment for my imagination!

As for the size of the Dust Vault, Snorkett had no idea. In all the forty-two years since his addictive visits began, he had only ever inhabited the area visible in the candlelight immediately in front of the door. Since the distance the light could travel was lessened by the dust-thick air, Garfield Snorkett's knowledge of the Vault was choked to what he now saw. Perhaps it's infinite, he had creduled at seventeen. Since his first visit he had found it necessary to reduce its boundaries to satisfy his claustrophilia.

Feeling queasy at the thought of accurate facts and figures, he now perceived the unknown space to be large-ish before turning his attention to more pressing matters.

'O Coral, come tonight, my little wife,' he crooned, and crouched to secure the candle in a mound of thick fluff which, as far as he could gather, coated the floor throughout: 'O Coral!'

The name jolted memories prematurely into Garfield's mind. Panicking, he yelped: 'No! Not yet. I'm not ready yet!' and began to undress, flinging each garment of clothing hotch-potch to the floor. Naked, he lay down beside the candle and with clots of dust from the floor covered his stomach and groin for decency's sake.

There. Ready.

He inhaled, filling his lungs with stale air and dust and then bellowed the forty-two year old command for the ceremony to begin.

'Now let me have Coral!'

Garfield lay motionless as images of his wife-as-she-was tripped towards him in succession: one dream one night one broken promise – YOU CORAL SNORKETT FORMERLY VAUGHAN NÉE SNORKETT ARE A GHOST OF YOUR FORMER SELF!

At seventeen years of age, he dreams of a girl he does not know: she dances before him, now clothed in white silk, now naked as the night. She dances in a moonlit field and in her hair is a chain of white lilies. The vague apparition skips into his arms and kisses his nose, smiling. Then the moon reddens and he cannot breathe. He struggles to break from her embrace but a silver cord has joined them navel-to-navel. The twins grapple in a tug o'war and in his frenzy he retches then weakens and submits as the girl smiles and persistently showers him in sororal kisses. They dance on in an incestuous womb of night.

At seventeen years of age, inspired by a dream, he searches for and finds the sister he never had. In the flickering candlelit darkness of an old air-raid shelter he tries to tell her she is his twin but, choked by her flirtatious beauty, allows her to seduce him. As they roll in the filth and dust she promises everlasting love: be mine, Snorkett begs – 'Always yours,' vows Coral.

At seventeen years of age he sees the promise broken when Coral is married to Dustin Vaughan. 'I meant what I said at the time,' is his sister's only defence to his angry rantings in the marquee at the wedding reception. Then she teases: 'You never know, though, keep your hopes up. I mean Dusty's nearly sixty and very nearly dead so think of all that money – you may just find a rich little Coral coming running back to you. Think about it. Not too long.' Garfield cries 'slut' and storms in tears from the tent amidst a babbling gossip of What Coral a slut that slip of a girl slutting not her never no slut? no.

When Garfield Snorkett is seventeen years old, the bottom drops out of reality and his spindly skinniness comes tumbling down once and for all to a soft-dust bed of memories in the tomb of his first and only love. And there he lies for forty-two years.

Now let me have Coral!

Images flooded Snorkett's senses: one dream-night-promise. And then faded, and he lay in the dust, exhausted and sweating, breathing shallow and quick. He awaited the return of his strength for the next stage of his ritual: resurrection of flesh and spirit – not remembering but reliving.

Voices leapt into the Dust Vault, followed by the yellow pulverulent tube of a torch beam, dancing over the dirt. It landed momentarily on Snorkett's foot. Shit! He leapt up, heart thumping, eyes agape, and flung a handful of dust on the candle to drown the flame. In the powdery pitch-blackness, he scrambled to collect his clothes before dashing from the light.

A boy and girl entered.

'Well, this is it,' said the boy, flashing his torch across the floor. 'What do you think?'

'I don't like it,' said the girl. She was trembling. 'It's filthy and I'm sure I saw a light in here as we came down the stairs – it's the dick that passed us on his scooter. I know it is.'

'Don't be stupid – we're alone. Come 'ere.'

Dick on a scooter? Thought Garfield, watching the two lovebirds he had overtaken earlier – moi? He had come to rest about ten feet from the door, praying that the light would not penetrate so far through the dust. He gazed on, curled up and quaking like a maltreated puppy. Nevertheless, he felt strangely touched by the gentle drama played out before him in the torchlight. It was blurred and darkened by the thick air, as vague as memory. And as disconcerting: dick on a scooter – me?

The boy and girl now lay side-by-side, silent except for the occasional snide remark or half-felt expression of love from the boy. Garfield noted that, gradually, the boy seemed to grow more impatient, fidgeting with the dust at his side. The girl had become insecure, and had shut her eyes tight, breathing nervously through slightly parted lips. Snorkett stared at the pretty shadowed face. He felt he could almost name the nameless girl. No prizes for guessing what I'd call her, he thought, just like me little . . . no!

He had noticed a hand clutched full of fluff, hovering above the shivering girl's face.

No, not dust in her face – not Coral's! Snorkett gasped as the hand opened and from it flopped a compressed lump of dust. The girl spluttered, screamed and struggled blindly as the boy bore down on top of her, laughing: 'Got you now, Lizzy, got you now!' She shrieked and pushed at him angrily, but he'd rolled his full weight onto her and soon she lay panting and mouthing no as the same hand impatiently tugged open her blouse, buttons springing off one by one, parting the material to pinch the shivering swell of white lace then slip it aside.

O Coral, we must stop him, we must, thought Snorkett. In a shock of envy he lurched snarling into the light to wrench the boy to his knees before cracking the lad's head against the wall.

'Just deserves, lecherous juvenile!' he screeched as the boy slumped unconscious to the ground. 'Let that be a lesson in the pains of love! Remember it, little shit!

'And now to you my sister memory – let me hold you.' He turned to gaze down at Coral but was blinded momentarily by the torch. 'Let me turn off your little light, sister-wife. We need no light.' Turning off the torch and placing it at arm's length he bent slowly down to the darkness where Coral lay. 'Your breasts, Coral – may I?' Head down, Garfy, you lucky bastard, slowly very slowly though and part lips moisten nice-and-moist no teeth gently and in-for-the-kill.

He sat up and spluttered, spitting a clot of dust from his mouth. 'What, Coral, where are you? Don't hide-and-seek from me. Not me. It's only me.'

He swept his hand through the dust beside him until he found the torch and, switching it on, lit the ground. Nothing. Nobody. No Coral. Just a small, slight indentation where her head had compressed the dust. Snorkett shivered, whined and choked as he fell forward, crying, 'No, Coral, not gone!'

He never noticed the quick footsteps growing fainter up the steps, nor even the groans of his younger self struggling to find consciousness. The angular fleshless creature just lay on his front, naked, sobbing into the mold of Coral's head. No, Coral, not gone.

Garfield Snorkett fell dustwards into a deep and dreamless sleep.

Confused? Then I'll expand. There is this place, you see, where the fifty-nine year old spindly skinniness of Garfield Snorkett now lies sleeping. It is a shelter or a dungeon or a tomb of some description whose floor, walls and ceiling are somehow coated with thick layers of filthy dust. Perhaps this venue does not suggest the setting for tragic love story – nevertheless it has long been a grave of romantic memories for our misfit of a romantic hero. Not for the real is this place, just for the surreal, Garfield used to sanctimoniously cry, nothing done, nothing explained, nothing really seen: just dreamt and . . . and . . . felt. That is how it should be and that is how it is. There is this place, you see, where

Garfield Snorkett now sleeps, this Dust Vault of memories, now somehow tainted by a lustful youth and a bared breast . . . you understand now? . . . or perhaps something doesn't quite gel.

The Malmers' special

You're kidding,' is the inevitable response I usually get when I tell folks about it now. And truth is it was the first thought that went through my mind back then. How the hell could they ask that of me?

But looking back, it was one of those opportunities that any pub chef worth his gravy would never pass up. When the four of them walked into the Rose and Crown that Wednesday lunchtime they were looking dead solemn. In fact, three of them were solemn, but one, the youngest, he just looked nervous, like he was about to cry.

They approached the bar in formation, one at the front, the rest in a row behind him. The one at the front, the oldest, looked a little more respectable than the rest. His shirt was ironed at any rate, while the rest blended better with my usual regulars.

'Hello,' he said.

'Gents,' I replied as I do, 'what can I do you for?'

'We're the Malmers, from Dewsbury,' he said as though it ought to mean something. 'We hear your pies are the best.'

'Oh,' I said, 'aye. We've got the lot, I boasted, pies being my speciality, my special little thing. Baked on the premises they are. It's a secret pastry recipe passed down from my great Aunt Gladys. You've taken a right little trek to get here but I can make sure your journey's been worthwhile. A veritable feast of fillings I've got, to suit all palates - steak 'n' ale, chicken 'n' mushroom in white wine sauce, free range pork with apple and spices -'

He cut me off.

'We have a request,' he said then placed an envelope on the bar. 'It's our late mother's last will and testament should show what we're after. You needn't read the lot, but you'll see on the second page that she's been quite specific about the disposal of her body.'

'Oh,' I said, not sure where he was going with this, but I figured we could do worse than have a few ashes scattered on the roses out the back. 'She was a regular then, was she?'

'Not at all,' said front Malmer as two of the rear Malmers shook their heads, 'she didn't get out. We're not that sort of family. Here, I'll read it to you.'

He removed the papers from the envelope, scanning through to find the relevant clause, then he read.

'I see,' I said when he'd finished, the old grey matter struggling to make sense of the words I'd just heard. *In honour of the close bond I have had with my four sons, all bachelors, now alone to fend for themselves, I would like to offer them one last gift while I still can.*

Just as my body sustained them as babes, I would have it do so again in death.

'I see,' I said. 'I see. I think I'm beginning to understand your interest in my pies.'

I think they saw that I was disgusted at first. There was obvious disappointment in their eyes and one of the rear Malmers looked ready to turn and leave, as though he'd seen it before. But pub food isn't what it used to be and I've been pushing the boundaries of classy nosh for so long now that my mind turned quickly to the practical side. Mushrooms and a nice red wine gravy? Or perhaps with a whisky sauce. That might be a bit on the rich side but you never know, although if she never went out perhaps it wouldn't be quite what she'd want. Simpler fare, perhaps. So many possibilities. Of course, I'd never really thought what old lady might taste like, although I did hear once that the fleshy bit at the base of the thumb can be a bit like chicken if cooked in a certain way. All four Malmers seemed to relax as we stood in silence, no doubt reassured by the grin I could feel had spread across my face.

But I was getting carried away, so I had to ask: 'Are you certain it was a pie she had in mind?'

The front Malmer nodded. The young nervy one licked his lips, then swallowed.

They returned next day to deliver mother Malmer. The four of them entered in the same formation a minute after I opened the doors at eleven. Their sombre mood from Wednesday had turned apprehensive and I wondered why. Perhaps they were worried

I'd bottle out on seeing what they'd brought. But it was all just ingredients really, wasn't it, already diced in an old ice cream tub. Walls Raspberry Ripple crossed out with marker pen, replaced with the family name in capitals, *MALMER*, and underneath, *MAM (for pie)*. I opened it a touch right away, enough to see what was in there. Just the right amount, I figured. I'd told them the necessary measure and it looked like they'd weighed it to the ounce. Steak diced, although I could chop it a bit smaller, and a measure of liver. And for the youngest of them who felt he'd lost the most, a few cubes of heart. His own request.

I made the pastry as normal, wondering for a moment what my great Aunt Gladys might have made of it. As for the filling, I settled on a simple onion sauce to complement the meat. No more than a touch of seasoning. I dare say the deceased wouldn't have wanted too much spice. I had that impression. And on Friday lunchtime, just after twelve, they returned and sat themselves at a corner table I'd set aside for them, all dressed half smart in nearly fitting suits, something funereal about them, saying nothing.

I serviced up, then brought the meals out two at a time, oldest and youngest Malmers first, then the other two. I'd laid out a good helping of thick buttery potato mash on each plate, a few roast parsnips, a serving of garden peas, a quarter of pie and a small ceramic pot of English mustard. Then I pulled half a pint of bitter apiece because a full one didn't seem right.

The brothers sat for a while, staring at their plates, not seeming to mind that I was watching them. They sat that way for a good five minutes and, just as I was getting anxious that their meals might go cold, the oldest Malmer picked up his knife and fork, and sighed.

'Right lads,' he said, 'here's to us and ours. Tuck in. Thanks, Mum.'

I watched it all, their edible wake. By turns they ate, laughed, cried, held each other. Do you remember the time she - oh but she left us wanting for nowt – took its toll when Dad left us all like that – aye the bastard - never raised a finger to us – oh such a woman she was – such a –

All four finished eating at the same time then fell silent again. They rose together and pushed in their chairs neatly. Then they filed out past me, each one nodding his gratitude, all except the youngest who stopped in front of me, his eyes moist.

'You got her just right. That's how she was,' he said, 'just like you did her, warm and right and tender. I've got her right here now, he said touching his heart. Right here.'

They return occasionally even now, two years on. No special recipes. They just sit in the corner at the same table, order fish and chips or the vegetarian pie, washed down with half a pint.

The suit whisperer

What would you do if they get out of hand? You must worry about that,' says Ben, not for the first time. It's his stock question. Anything to get me feeling jumpy before the rush hour starts. He thinks I'm mad, herding the suits without a prod.

We're sitting in our rest room at the north end of the platform, me slurping tea, Ben shovelling his fourth heap of sugar, chiming the edge of his mug with the spoon.

'They're fine,' I say, 'you just got to know how to play them.'

Ben grins. 'I've herded these platforms for fourteen years. I know how to play the buggers,' he says resting his hand over the black plastic tip of his prod, teasing the red button, grinning. 'Why would anyone do it different?'

I say nothing, but my answer is behind him. A crayon picture of me drawn by my five-year-old. I'm smiling in it, surrounded by grinning suits which I'm guiding safely to their carriage, ushering them merrily on board. The caption reads: *dady helps sots + scerts*. She's scrawled her name in the bottom left, Lucy, set in a large orange heart.

'There are gentler ways,' I say to Ben.

'Yeah yeah,' he smirks. 'Gentler ways that'll get you crushed if you don't watch it.'

There was a time when I sympathised with Ben, when I carried my own prod to keep the herd in line. Not just a prod even. I kept a chain on my belt too, sometimes, to jangle at them because of how they hate that sound, but more often than not to swing at them them when they ignored the prod. But that isn't how I want to get along. I might have risen up the ranks, as Ben likely will, doing the same as all the other herders each morning and night, but it's Lucy I have to think of now.

The alarm sounds. The next lot is due.

'Bastard,' moans Ben. 'I've barely touched my drink. Your phone time right?'

'Afraid so,' I say, standing to peer through the small wire meshed glass in the door. I can see the first few suits are gathering on the platform. There's a skirt at the end too. A young thing. Ben's seen her.

'How about that one for a grab? Reckon, eh?'

With that, he's off out the door, leaving me to steal a last sip of tea. He unclips his prod, waving it in the air, screaming, 'Get out of it you lazy fucks, you know the drill, behind the fucking yellow line, get the fuck, you trying to get your fucking selves killed, train's fucking coming fucks, it's fucking coming in a fucking minute, fucking move.' The skirt flinches as he approaches. She's met him before, I can tell from her panic, although whether he's been further than just met I can't be sure. Perhaps one of the many he's tried to work in his way, a little more than the herding he was hired for. 'Keeps them tame,' he's said often enough and maybe he's right. 'Gets the respect I need for me and my prod.'

I have to admit Ben's no worse than most. Better than plenty. The skirts could do worse.

I walk slowly onto the platform, the suits at this end hardly noticing, only swaying a little as they begin to sense me. None are looking across. Not at first. Not until a lanky one a few metres away gives me a sideways glance, sways a little more. His hands instinctively rise to his skewed tie. They do that sometimes, I've never known why. He straightens it, tightens it a little. I lower my head. Never gaze straight at them, not until I know. He glances again, then looks away. Then again and this time he keeps looking as I raise my head, look him straight in the eye. I nod, smile, and then I know. He's my seed. That's all it takes. Just one to grow trust from the others.

He's the one Ben would have prodded first, for that first sideways look. 'You fucking looking at, you fuck?' That's all the suit would have known before yelping at the voltage jolting his ribs, head, groin. 'Give them the holy fucking trinity, send them double and you can't go wrong.' The suit's yelp would send ripples through the others around him, immediate fear of the prod, of Ben. Immediate compliance.

But there are gentler ways to herd suits, no matter what Ben reckons. The lanky one's glance showed me he's more aware than the rest. For Ben, a glance is a provocation. For me, it's an opening.

I've often thought about getting out of this game. But I'm thirty-nine and this is all I know. I've worked other stations, all similar to this one. It doesn't really matter whether you're herding suits and skirts into carriages here or carriages elsewhere. The job changes little from place to place. They have to be sent. But it'd be good to see a bit of daylight occasionally. Even the suits get that, as they pass through, doing their thing up there, whatever it is they have them do. But me, I'm down here through the daylight hours. By the time I come up for home, there's nothing left of the day and little left of me. I've given it all to the suits. I'll head back to the apartment, wander into Lucy's room, watch her sleep a while, then if I have some energy perhaps I'll nudge our own skirt awake, have some moments with her before I sleep myself, dreaming of the suits' dull faces, their rare sparks of recognition. Then I'll wake, head back underground again. To Ben and his prod.

The rush has started. The steady flow of suits, the occasional skirt, spilling onto the platform. Ben's wielding his prod like a sword, roaring at them. 'Down the other fucking end, fuckers,' he's screaming. 'Use the full fucking length of the platform.' As always, their memories too short to recall the morning rush they fail to respond until he prods one or two. The shrieks send others surging to wherever Ben would have them. But he's pissed off about something. I think he lost his skirt in the crowd. Not for the first time. Losing his chance of a bit always pisses him off.

My seed is still gazing at me, the tired dark of his eyes searching for something in me. I trust he'll not let me down. In that moment, in the depths of the crowd in the depths of this terminal I know he'd be lost without me. I nod again, to be sure. His hands rise to his throat, adjusting his tie again in nervous salute.

There's a rush of tepid air along the platform, the lights of the next train approaching from deep in the tunnel. The suits begin to surge to the platform edge, that urge to be so close they might touch the carriages as they come to a halt.

'Back, get back, you dense fucks,' Ben is shouting. 'Hear me? Get back.'

But I don't shout and warn. I just mouth 'No' to my seed, as those around him begin to jostle. 'No.'

He lets out a guttural moan. Mournful. It always is, and the jostling stops immediately. The suits turn and look at my seed, lean in slow towards him as he repeats the moan.

'What are you fucking doing, you fucks?' screams Ben from the other end of the platform at the figures jostle around him. I can barely hear him above the sound of the train. Poking and prodding them for all he's worth. All the while trying to position himself with one of the skirts. Any of them. Before it's too late. Before they're boarded and gone. It's his entertainment, that panic of pursuit.

The train slows and stops and the suits start boarding the empty carriages. I calm them from rushing with a gentle hand on a shoulder or a whisper of nothing in particular.

But there's no sign of Ben. Suits of all ages pushing towards the same carriage door. There must be fifty of them, speechless, shouldering each other.

Where is the idiot? Most likely shoved into a carriage. It wouldn't be the first time. I know he'll be back in the morning with claims of how he pulled that skirt, or some other. But I saw the rush so I doubt today's trip was intentional. All that's left of him is his prod, discarded on the floor where he dropped it. I'll fetch it later.

The train pulls away, and even before it's rumble has faded, the first of a new herd wander onto the platform. An elderly skirt pauses by Ben's prod, sways a moment as though something isn't right, then walks on.

You and Rick Wilson

I've an urge to slap you for looking at my Rick like that. You'll understand, I'm sure. But we're fine for now. He needs his fun. Perhaps so do you. I'll not get in your way, but you'll excuse me if I watch from over here as you sidle to his end of the bar to be closer. Brush hands. Accidentally. Eyes meet. You do that smile. And you think you're the predator. How sweet, when if you look at the bar top you'll likely see two decades of scratches from false nails like yours, left by girls clawing their way over, seeing fit to be snug with my Rick Wilson.

He sits there at the bar most nights with a look on his face that makes you want to know what he knows. Given the chance and a beer and a few minutes of your time he'll begin his play. He loves to share himself with young things like you. His once-upon-a. His you'll-never-guess-what. His here's-how-life-is-for-me.

He's likely older than your father. Is that why you want him?

And by turns he's making you laugh, making you melt, giving you butterflies, but his dimpled cheeks are turning you maternal, and I can tell you haven't quite figured that one out, how you actually don't mind.

And for him. Oh, the thrill. That smell of young. That freshness. You're no threat, but you are, so I can't stop watching. The chance he might give you a smile too deep, a wink too many. That I can't and mustn't risk that. It's not you as such, but the newness of it. And if he ever did follow through, I really don't know what I'd do.

He's unlikely to mention his old teacher to you. Miss Jace. Fresh out of college. So naïve. I wonder if he still thinks of her, how he had her put her hand down his pants when he was fourteen years old. Why would a teacher do that, you'd ask, if you hadn't met Rick. But you know him now, so I daresay you can imagine. Poor woman, Miss Jace. But so are we all, and I can't paint us all as victims. She deserved everything she got for that touch. He might have offered freely, but she stole even so.

For an extra smile he'll get you into the lock-in after hours. You're all good, he'll say. Great, you'll say. There'll be just him and you, a few others, me of course, snug over here, and the landlord, throwing me an uneasy glance: no scenes tonight, please. I can tell that even with the place all but empty that you haven't seen me watching. But then, be honest, you haven't noticed a thing since you first laid eyes. There's just you and Rick Wilson, the dull hum of the jukebox speaker lost behind his song, so smooth, his charm never faltering, his stories never frilled or veering.

Were you a prettier woman, a slimmer one, perhaps less pimpled, more subtly made up, you might notice Rick slipping his hand in his trouser pocket as he talks. You might notice a gentle stroke beneath the pleat of his suit trouser. There's not many men who could get away with that. Most would get called for a pervert. But Rick, my Rick, he'd only steal your attention more. But you aren't prettier, slimmer or less pimpled, and your skin under the weight of your pasted-on designer grease looks altogether orange in this light, so he'll only go so far with you. Still, you've piqued his interest, so be grateful for that, while I watch relieved as his hands don't leave his pint glass.

He'll be telling you of his business dealings, trips along the South Coast, over to Europe. The people he met there. That's deliberate. That pinch of jealousy you felt just now because you think you know that by people he meant other women. But you needn't worry. I'm the one who should be jealous, the only woman who ever owned him, now drowning in his words, gagging at each drop of them, reassured only slightly by the fact that everything he's saying is fantasy. It's the life he would have had. Were it not for. Well, he needs his moment. He needs to impress, and he does it well. Lets him feel like a man. Like a dog needs to walk unleashed when the time and place are right, so I let him off every evening or so, to sniff the likes of you.

You're off to the ladies now, saying hold that thought, be right back. You'll be thinking to adjust yourself. Scent yourself. Perhaps linger by the machine in there for a moment, wondering should you or whether he has already. But no, you'll be thinking, you don't want anything to dull the warmth between you and him, to plug his flow, to sully the feel of him, not even a slight skin of rubber. So you return with nothing.

The bar falls silent and Rick pauses a moment too long before looking across at me. I don't like that delay. Do the other drinkers sense that? The landlord does. He's looking from you to me, then back again.

What's on my Rick's mind now? Perhaps we're all wondering, you as well, and I catch myself hoping you've overdone your scent, that with your stuck-on nails you've accidentally burst a pimple, that your pus will turn his stomach, somehow, anyhow, because I don't know what I'd do if he left. I don't.

I wait until you're right in front of him, wondering if you should giggle and stroke that ruffled hair of his into place, before I clear my throat. Rick ignores me at first, wanting to wait for what you'll do next. He's after another little while with you. Perhaps more. Perhaps I've misread. I do it again, rasp at the both of you.

'I think I'll be calling time now, Rick,' I say, louder than intended, shuddering. What's on his mind?

You peer at me through the gloom. Yes, there is another woman in here with you. Don't look so surprised. Rick's posture slumps and I know we'll be alright. He doesn't give you another glance. Nor will he. You've had your free drinks. That's your perk, a few tall stories and his attention. But I'll have him now, my Rick, and look at that, good as gold he's heading back to my side, trying not meet my gaze.

'Evening, Mrs Wilson,' calls the barman, with an edge in his voice that says he'd like us to leave. 'We'll see you tomorrow?'

I look at Rick Wilson: 'Oh, I should think so.'

And Rick Wilson says to me: 'May I help you up, Mother?'

At which I feel your eyes on me. Oh, what did you expect, girl? Even a charmer like Rick Wilson has his Mother.

We walk out and a strong wind whips our faces as we stumble through the dark to the cottage. I squeeze his hand, dig my nails, to say slow down, savour it, where's the rush?

'Dirty slut, that one,' I say.

My Rick nods but says nothing. You're out of his mind. One hand he slips into mine, the other he slips into his pocket.

Angel caging

X Factor was on the last time it happened.

'It rapes carpets. Nice pedal,' said Mags.

It wasn't what she was trying to say. Not nearly. Not again, she thought.

Trevor didn't hear. He had the television up loud and her words sank deep beneath the judges' banter. She reached for his hand, as he stroked at the worn velvet on the arm of his chair, but she missed by a finger and her hand flopped into the gulf between them. His eyes were fixed on the tanned, toothy judge. The smiley one. Damn, if Mags could just lean to him a bit further and reach his hand, but she could barely move when she went like this. And on the telly, those teeth. Trevor wide-eyed. He'd not be looking Mags' way anytime soon.

'Towelling,' said Mags, bitterly. Please not now, she thought. The words in her head lined up, ready for her mouth, and spilled out as nonsense, someone else writing the script.

She'd been in town first time it happened, at Pharm-a-tastic, collecting Trevor's meds for his ears. She said something about jelly, smiling as the sales woman took her money. She'd meant it as a compliment. New hair style. Orange streaks. Striking. But it came out as jelly. The woman stared at Mags for a moment, then burst out laughing. A young couple in the queue behind her joined the giggling when Mags tried to repeat herself and made even less sense.

Of course, they all had a laugh about it the following Sunday. Well, Trevor did, when they bumped into Bessie and George before the service at St Michael's. Mags kept quiet. She had nothing to add.

'She's always talked nonsense,' said Trevor, 'and there's not a lot we can say to each other after forty-one years.'

Bessie cackled at that.

'True, true,' hooted George, 'I can't remember the last time I listened to Bessie.'

'Cheeky bugger,' said Bessie.

'Somebody say something?' said George, and the three of them cracked up, Bessie nudging his arm hard, spilling his pint.

'Oh you,' she said.

Trevor winked at Mags, raised his glass. She smiled stiffly.

'It's part of growing old,' he said later, as they walked home. Mags' arm was looped in his. Was this him trying to be understanding? 'It's part of that long decay. Skin rips easier. Bruises last longer. Everything aches. Your ears go, well, you know how my ears have gone? And you've always been the daft one. That right?'

The X Factor judges were grilling some poor contestant when Mags tried to reach for Trevor's hand again: 'Do the world a favour: stop singing today,' quipped the too-tanned judge on the right, the one everyone loved to hate. Mags could barely raise her hand. She gave up.

'Able mean took,' said Mags, all but shouting for Trevor's attention, her mouth dry, throat rasping. The room had turned double. It didn't usually go on this long. She'd always been back to herself by now. The television. So loud. Unbearable.

The audience booed the last judge as the rejected contestant slunk off, stocky, unshaven, broke.

'I'm with the judges,' Trevor called at the man. 'Someone should've told you. Do the world a favour. Really, do you not think, Mags? Someone should have told him. Do you not think?'

'Angel caging,' she replied, 'that meat.'

Turn and look at me, she thought. Please. At least she could gesture if he'd only look, twitch her hands, shudder her head or something. But his gaze didn't leave the television.

At one point, months ago, she tried to talk to a doctor about it. She phoned at any rate, but it was emergencies only until Thursday and there was something in the receptionist's tone that made her think it would be best to wait. Besides, Mags felt fine at the time. It wasn't important. She only felt a bit of a wobble in her head afterward, whenever it happened, but apart from that she was no less normal than always. Just part of growing old, like Trevor said. But frightening. So frightening. Locked in like this.

How many times now? She'd lost count. Eight, maybe. Nine.

'Don't get up, I'll make you a cup of tea,' Trevor said when the advertisements came on.

'Drizzle,' Mags whispered, as her husband left the room.

Mumma smudge

It was messed up. That's what it was. Waiting here for Stev to get back with the parts, the twitching mess in the copier tray, its owner flapping around trying to organise her life, and her kid, the boy, who couldn't be more than two or three, running around like it happened every day. Maybe it did for all I knew.

'Mumma smudge,' said the boy. He did one of those pantomime shrugs that kids' entertainers do. 'Oopsie. Mumma smudge,' he said again, looking across at his mum in the hallway then back at the bloodied smudge, naked in the copier out-tray.

The kid's mum wasn't even looking. She was losing her rag on the phone. 'He's your son too, Bradley,' she hissed, 'please, the engineers are here – well one engineer and I think the other's a trainee, he's just hanging around like a – and I'm run ragged and I have to get off, I just need you to –'

I tried to smile at the boy, knowing full well that even at the best of times my smiles make me look like I'm constipated.

Oopsie. Poor sod. Maybe this did happen every day. Maybe he had no clue from one day to the next whether it was his hyper stressed real mum and dad looking out for him and putting him to bed, or a three-day unlicensed copy from this second-hand machine.

'Head,' he said, his finger almost poking the smudge's face. The thing in the out-tray looked terrified. No surprise really. It most likely had all the memories of the original. Chances are this one knew exactly what was about to happen. There'd be none of the three days of everyday stuff, taking a bit of pressure off real mum in the hall out there. No humane fade to blue that the brochures claimed each copy felt, as its memories were merged with its owner's. This one knew it only had Stev's bolt to the back of its head to look forward to in a few minutes.

'Sure,' I said, 'head.'

'Daddy, hi,' said the kid's mum in the hallway, 'yes yes, of course I'm fine, yes yes, of course, yes, listen Daddy, listen – actually, I'm not. Bradley's a shit, Daddy, and we've got another smudge – what? – it's what everyone calls them. The copier has jammed, Daddy. I have a meeting in town and daycare is full so I made a copy to mind Travis – I don't know what went wrong. It's disgusting, Daddy. Bloody thing – would you? Bradley and his cheap cartridge deals. Oh, bless you, Daddy – yes, I know you would but I don't like to ask, you know, with Mummy like she is, and the copies usually –'

Shitsake. What was taking Stev so long? Strangers' homes in the middle of a copier breakdown. Nothing was worse. I should have run for the tools myself.

The kid crouched next to the smudge in the tray.

'Don't look at it,' I said to him. He was staring at its lower torso, twisted and cut where it connected with the copier, as though the machine was eating not spewing it out. The kid turned to the smudge's face and he smiled. It looked back at him, and of all the messed-up things its body calmed, convulsions fading. Only its arm still twitched as it tried to lift it to touch the boy's face. So messed up.

'Mumma nice smudge.'

'Yeah, listen,' I said, 'please piss off to the other room, kid. This is too screwed up. This mess isn't your mumma. It's not nothing, and my mate's going to be back in a sec and he…oh, this is too screwed up.'

But he had already lent forward to kiss its cheek, like he was kissing it goodnight. Did he know what was about to happen? I could hear Stev bumping the bag of heavy tools against the front door as he struggled into the apartment at last.

'Look, the other one's your mumma, mate,' I said, 'this one's just meat. Go and give your real mumma a cuddle.'

But the little bastard didn't budge. He held the smudge's twitching hand. It gave a weak smile and closed its eyes as the boy went to kiss it again.

Jeremy
in mauve

Tina's on her way to the window table to take the bloke's order. She doesn't want to because she knows she's going to laugh, but Mary's been prancing round him for ages, snapping photos on her phone and sticking them on Instagram. Nick the manager jokes about throwing him out.

'What's with him? Can't be doing with it,' he laughs, 'he's in the window, see what I mean. He'll scare people off.'

But Tina figures someone has to do his order, so she's on her way over, notebook flipped open, the imprint of the last order pressed through from the previous page: all day big breakfast, coffee, extra fried bread.

She's going to laugh. She can feel it. And she can feel Mary watching, poised with her phone, ready to start clicking. Her photo will be all over the internet before she gets back to the kitchen. She wonders what a guy who dresses like that even eats, sitting there, reading the sports page with a look so serious across his heavy, unshaven face. She looks from his tattered, laceless walking boots, to the crinkled flesh coloured stockings that barely mask his tangled leg hair, to the plunge of a mauve floral print cotton dress that barely conceals his chest hair.

Tina's going to laugh at the bloke. She knows it.

୰

Norm thinks he knows the guy. What is he? Late thirties. Early forties. He could have been at school with him, and that in itself makes his skin crawl.

He remembers Pete from the yard telling him about a trip to Phuket where he hooked up with this woman, dead fit he said, only to get her back to his room and unwrap a pair of fake breasts and a shaved cock and balls. So messed up. But this? Norm can't work out whether this is worse or not. There's no disguise. The guy isn't hiding a thing, sitting there with three days' growth on his chin and wearing a bloody purple dress. Jesus wept.

The waitress, the nice one, June, Sarah, something, is taking the bloke's order. 'Just a cup of tea, love, please, oh and a round of buttered toast would be smashing,' says the bloke, as though everything's normal.

Norm tries to match the guy's face with mental mugshots of old schoolmates. With one less layer of fat he thinks it could be Wilson. Nah. Maybe? But Wilson was straight as they come. Maybe you can't tell. Damn. Norm can't stomach his fried bread. He pushes his plate away.

୬

Danny's trying not to hold Mum's hand as they enter the cafe.

He wants to run to the table by the window so he can watch the cars outside. That's what they always do when they eat in here. But Mum's holding him back, and anyway there's a fat old woman sitting there. Danny can see under the table between her parted legs. He can see right up her dress, her legs wide apart like Dad always sits, and when he squints he's sure he can see a pair of England boxer shorts.

No way. He tugs at Mum's hand.

'Mum,' he whispers.

But Mum's dragging him to the table by the toilets.

'You haven't been since we left the house,' she says, gently.

'Mum,' he says again.

'Wait,' she warns, but smiles as she waggles her finger before reaching for the menu. 'Sit nicely,' she says. 'Chicken nuggets or fish fingers?'

Danny stares at the old lady, trying to see her underpants again, but he can't.

୬

Rosie is stuck sweltering in her car in the jam on the high street. She mutters at a woman who lets her Tesco bag bump the passenger door as she walks past. Silly cow. Then there he is, looking up at her from his newspaper, his round face spreading into a smile.

Good grief, she thinks, wondering for a moment if she's seeing what she thinks she is, or if it's some trick in the window reflection. No. He really is wearing that dress. Her anger fades, becomes something quite different.

Is he, does he always, I mean, she wonders. That a man like him can dress like that, even round here. It's. She doesn't know what it is, but it's somehow, well, liberating. Just seeing him.

She tries to soften her eyes, smile extra wide, so he knows she's with him, she's really with him. Her. Is he a her? A woman trapped in a – yes, her. She'll think of him as her. If she was in the cafe right now, or even walking by, she's not sure, but she thinks she might hug him. Her.

'Oi, sweetheart.' It's the driver of the car behind her, hanging half out of his window, banging his roof to get her attention. Oh, she thinks, noticing the gap between her and the car in front. She pulls away, turning to wave at that beautiful, amazing, soulful woman in the café window.

Nice girl, thinks Jeremy. He waves back as she drives away, and then folds his paper. He doesn't much care for tennis.

He glances round the café at people trying not to stare, and makes eye contact with the man at the back. Jeremy nods. The man turns away. He knows what people are thinking and it doesn't bother him. He's heard the same thoughts often enough in his own head.

The young lad sitting with his mum pulls tongues at him. Jeremy pulls tongues back. The boy giggles, hiding behind his hands. Never hide, thinks Jeremy.

'You finished?' asks the waitress. Not the one who took his order. The other one. The one who was taking pictures.

'Thank you, I am,' he replies. He reads her name tag: 'But Mary, just a moment. Perhaps you'd like to...?'

He motions with his hands, hoping she'll get what he means, which she does. She smiles, reaches into her pocket, crouches beside him, and angles the phone camera so their faces fill the screen. I should have shaved, he thinks, pouting. The waitress laughs, pouting too, leaning into him. The camera clicks.

Acknowledgements

Authors of short fiction often find they've earned themselves the slightly odd label of *emerging author*. This can be a badge of honour while we're getting our first few publications out there, but the novelty wears off quickly.

So, having had forty-six short and tiny pieces of fiction published I figured it might be time to finally *emerge* (whatever that means) by bringing some of those previously published pieces together in a single volume. Hence this book.

If this doesn't officially mean I've *emerged*, if that's even a thing, at least my stuff's a bit easier to find now.

Many thanks to the following publishers and publications (some well established, some obscure, some still going, some sadly defunct) that have taken a punt on my work over the past decade or so and offered first homes to the stories in this collection...

Andromeda Spaceways Inflight Magazine, The Battered Suitcase, Bridge House, BULL: Men's Fiction, Byker Books, Critical Quarterly, Dogmatika, elimae, Everyday Fiction, Foundling Review, HISSAC, Ink Sweat & Tears, Litro, The Northville Review, Parasitic, Prick of the Spindle, The Pygmy Giant, Radio Wildfire, Red Peter, Sparks, Tales of the Decongested and Vagabondage Press.

A note on the author

Martin Reed lives in London with his partner and two children. He works for The Society of Authors and is currently editing his first novel and drafting a second. His short fiction has been published widely in print and online.

Angel Caging is his first collection.

www.IamMartinReed.co.uk
@IamMartinReed

© Chloe Reed 2016

16777966R00082

Printed in Poland
by Amazon Fulfillment
Poland Sp. z o.o., Wrocław